"Whe   **t**
waste

"You'd b   place restored and open for business." One corner of her mouth tilted up, and if he wasn't mistaken, that was the fire of determination in her eyes. "Bet on it."

He crossed his arms over his chest and leaned closer. "I don't have to. This is my place. My father's already promised to let me give it a shot. I'm going to make my changes on my own timeline. You lose."

Her lips tightened and she closed her eyes for two seconds. "Of course. You're right. I'd forgotten in the excitement of seeing the place." She stepped back. "Thank you for the tour."

She held out her hand. Dean reluctantly shook it. Surely it couldn't be this easy.

Then she smiled at his father. "When this fails, Mr. Collins, please give me a call. As long as the building's still standing, I'm interested in having my chance."

Dear Reader,

Have a seat in one of the rocking chairs on the front porch of the Bluebird Bed-and-Breakfast and enjoy the view of Spring Lake. Right now the whole place can use some tender loving care, but Robert Collins has a plan for that. His son, Dean, a famous photojournalist, or Dr. Elaine Watson, the busiest, best doctor in town, will give the place a face-lift.

Elaine's plan involves restoration, a return to the Bluebird she remembers from happy family vacations. Dean is preparing for an overhaul. He's looking for adventure and an escape from his painful memories.

Tall Pines, Spring Lake, and this bed-and-breakfast are a mixture of places I've visited or wish I could someday. I hope you enjoy your visit! If your first trip to Tall Pines was *A Minute on the Lips*, you'll have a chance to catch up with Mark and Andi, too.

If you'd like to know more about my books and what's coming next, enter fun giveaways, or meet my dog, Jack, please visit me at cherylharperbooks.com. You can sign up for my newsletter, too. I'm also on Facebook (CherylHarperRomance) and Twitter (@CherylHarperBks). I'd love to chat!

Cheryl Harper

HEARTWARMING

The Bluebird Bet

———

Cheryl Harper

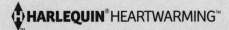

Recycling programs
for this product may
not exist in your area.

ISBN-13: 978-0-373-36716-0

The Bluebird Bet

Copyright © 2015 by Cheryl Harper

Printed in U.S.A.

Cheryl Harper discovered her love for books and words as a little girl, thanks to a mother who made countless library trips and an introduction to Laura Ingalls Wilder's Little House stories. Whether it's the prairie, the American West, Regency England or Earth a hundred years in the future, Cheryl enjoys strong characters who make her laugh. Now Cheryl spends her days searching for the right words while she stares out the window and her dog, Jack, snoozes beside her. And she considers herself very lucky to do so.

For more information about Cheryl's books, visit her online at cherylharperbooks.com or follow her on Twitter, @cherylharperbks.

Books by Cheryl Harper

HARLEQUIN HEARTWARMING

A Minute on the Lips

Visit the Author Profile page
at Harlequin.com for more titles.

CHAPTER ONE

"LOOKS LIKE YOU'VE been getting plenty of sun, Mr. Collins," Elaine Watson murmured as she looked over his vitals. "That might be good for your blood pressure but not your skin." She glanced over her glasses to see Robert Collins roll his eyes over a sunburned nose.

"I'm old, Doc. I'll risk a little burn to feel the sun on my face."

"Skin cancer is no joke," Elaine answered and realized what a bossy know-it-all she sounded like. But she'd seen countless families suffer through the disease, and she didn't want to watch Robert Collins do the same. He was her favorite patient.

Then she remembered that he'd lost his wife to cancer and realized what a waste of breath lecturing him was. He'd already lived through the worst. No one could forget that.

"Just try some sunscreen while you're out on Spring Lake, okay? For my sake." He nodded once, and she decided to believe he was agreeing with her instead of moving the conversation along.

"Any new complaints? You've lost another ten pounds, so whatever you're doing is working." Elaine flipped through his chart. When he'd arrived at the after-hours emergency care center two years ago, he'd been in bad shape with chest pains and blood pressure through the roof. His improvement was thanks to an angioplasty and medication to control his blood pressure combined with a desire to make a change.

"Fit as a fiddle, Doc. In fact, I'm about to take more of your advice. I'm going to get a new hobby. Bet you never thought you'd see the day." Noting the gleam in his eyes, Elaine braced herself. A teasing Robert Collins was a charming, dangerous thing.

When they'd first met, getting him to talk about anything had felt like an accomplishment. Over time, this strong, silent type had thawed.

Elaine set his chart down. "Hit me with

it. I can't wait to hear what piece of life-saving advice has trickled in."

"I'm going to travel." He stuck out his chin as if she'd pin a star to his chest if they handed out medals for good ideas. "Gonna get one of those high-class travel trailers and see some purple mountains and gold waves of grain and white, sandy beaches."

"Really?" Elaine tilted her head as she considered the suggestion. "By yourself?"

Robert frowned. "If I have to. You don't think I can?" It was an insult he would never stand for. Even after all they'd been through, he had a hard time believing he was no longer bulletproof.

She studied his clear eyes, shining with intelligence and a little bit of annoyance, thought about his vitals and then nodded. "Sure. You can. Do you *want* to?"

He snorted. "What difference does it make? I'm out there all by myself every day. Gets old after a while. A change of scenery would be a nice thing."

Too much alone time was something Elaine understood. Sometimes being by herself was wonderful. At the end of every day, she needed some silence to catch her breath. Other times, it was lonely. Lately, a restless dissatisfaction had intruded on her quiet. But nothing would tempt her away from Robert's spot on the lake if she was lucky enough to own it.

"You mean the prettiest view of Spring Lake and the mountains around Tall Pines isn't enough?" Elaine tapped her pen. "I'm not sure I can imagine anything better than sitting on the porch of the Bluebird Bed-and-Breakfast."

"You haven't been out to the inn for years, Doc. Been more than a decade since Martha died and the place…" He stared at his folded hands. "It's not what it used to be. Until recently, I couldn't stand the thought of changing anything."

Elaine patted his shoulder. This was the biggest challenge of treating her patients: knowing what to say or do when absolutely nothing she said or did would ease the pain. Some hurts only time would heal. No doubt losing his wife would make it difficult to enjoy the view from the wraparound porch of the Bluebird Bed-and-Breakfast. Maybe Elaine couldn't imagine anything better than a rocking chair and the calm of Spring

Lake after a hard day, but she didn't have his memories, either.

A single rocking chair might not be as satisfying as she tried to convince herself it could be.

"I should have hit the road years ago. Might have been easier to deal with losing her." His choked voice said clearly that nothing in the world would make losing his wife any easier. Elaine hated to hear that pain even as she wondered if she'd ever find someone who'd miss her that much when she was gone.

"Mr. Collins, you're on the right track. The best part is that if your trip isn't what you dream of, you can always come home to Tall Pines. This place will still be here, Spring Lake will still have some of the best fishing in the state and we've got plenty of mountains, too." The fact that Tall Pines changed slowly was one of its finest features. Life moved quickly. People came and went, most of them before she was ready to say goodbye, so a place like this was ideal.

She tried an encouraging smile that must have worked, because the sadness on his face drained away.

"What are you going to do with the Bluebird? I spent some great summers there, so if you're thinking of selling, I'd love to make an offer."

At that moment, anyone checking Elaine's pulse would definitely be concerned. She'd been working and saving forever without any notion what she was hoping for.

Now she knew. This inn was meant to be hers.

The frown that wrinkled his brow was unusual. No matter how sad he might be, Robert Collins always smiled. The day he'd walked into the emergency clinic with chest pains, he'd led with a joke and done his best to keep the mood light while the nurses scurried around him.

"Well, now, here's the problem." He sighed. "You remember Dean, right?"

"Sure. Vaguely." Dean Collins was a few years older than she was. He'd been around the Bluebird Bed-and-Breakfast the summers she'd visited, but neither one of them had taken much notice of the other. To her, he'd always seemed so wild and mysterious. "And I've seen some of his work." She was going to leave it at that. A son who would let his father recover from heart surgery alone didn't rate very high in her book even if he'd won awards for his photography. No matter how she struggled to manage her mother's wild mood swings, she'd never desert her.

"Well, he's in town. Showed up out of the blue last week, moved into his old bedroom like he hadn't been gone and announced he wants to reopen the inn." He shook his head. "Just like that. I was surprised, to say the least."

She was, too. The ache of disappointment that settled in her chest was silly. She hadn't even had a chance to buy the Bluebird, much less actually lose one.

Don't be so emotional, Elaine. He's been planning to leave it to his son, of course. That's what families do. There's no need to take it personally.

She forced a smile. "Well, that's good, then. You won't have to worry about the Bluebird while you're seeing America the beautiful." And she'd keep on working, saving her money for who knows what, and ignore the strange dissatisfaction that was getting harder to shake even with double emergency shifts and crazy office days.

Robert Collins moved his head back and forth as if he wasn't quite as convinced. "Except he's proven more than once that this is not where he wants to be. He's gotten tight-lipped with all this travel, so I haven't managed to figure out where the change of heart is coming from, but I'm afraid to trust it."

A discreet tap on the door by Nina, Elaine's dedicated nurse, signaled the end of their appointment. Patients were waiting in the other exam rooms, and the lobby was a madhouse. Resigned that the day had to march on, Elaine stood up and said, "Maybe he'll stay until you're ready to see Spring Lake again."

Robert Collins slid off the exam table. "Here's the thing. It's a tough decision, but it's the right time. Someone else can take the Bluebird and make it special again. Martha would want that, and she'd want me to get off my hindquarters and do something with all this time. Running an inn... well, I think maybe it's a talent a person's born with. Martha had that gift—it ran in

her blood. Without her, the business just…
stopped. The place lost its magic, and eventually guests stopped coming. That suited
me fine for a while. Now, I'm not sure
Dean's the right choice, but I don't know
if I can let it go to someone else." Robert
blinked slowly. "I understand that letting it
fall down around my ears is the worst option. Martha'd hate to see her inn looking
like it does."

Elaine squeezed his arm. "Let Dean take
a shot. What's the worst that could happen?"

Nothing felt comfortable about this
whole situation, but it seemed like the right
thing to say. She wanted the Bluebird. She
should make him an offer. But he wanted
the best for his son and for the Bluebird.
She would encourage him, even if it went
against her nature.

"You surprise me, Doc. Figured a take-
no-prisoners winner would seize any weakness." He raised an eyebrow. "Better not let
Wanda Blankenship see that soft under-
belly when the Fourth of July half marathon comes around. She'll knock you out
of the top spot."

Oh, no. She would not. Elaine had placed first in the women's division every year since she'd moved here. Wanda Blankenship, owner of the town gym, would eat her dust again this year.

Some of her warrior's spirit must have shown on her face because Robert laughed as though it was the funniest thing in the world to put a target on Wanda Blankenship's back. Good thing he wasn't racing.

"You have to do what you believe is right, Mr. Collins. I'm doing my best not to launch into a hard sell, mainly because I like you so much." Elaine rested her hand on the doorknob. "You know how I feel. I spent some lovely afternoons on the front porch drinking tea with my mother. I'd love to have that view of Spring Lake as my own."

Robert nodded slowly. "Well, how about…" He stared off into space for a second and then nodded again. "Come out for a visit. Meet Dean. We'll talk about your plans and then see…" He shrugged. "Maybe selling to you is the best thing for me and Dean. Maybe he needs somewhere to catch his breath before he hits the road again. I don't want a run-down building holding him back any more than I want to be the one keeping the Bluebird from being restored. Once he sees I've got a buyer, he might see the benefit of coming up with a new plan."

"He could hit the road with you. You could see the country together." Elaine couldn't help it. She should encourage this plan. Robert Collins might be one of her favorite people, but his son was fair game. She could outmaneuver him without the slightest guilt.

Maybe.

"Right." Robert rubbed his forehead. "We don't usually see eye to eye. Once his mother died, Tall Pines lost all hold on him, and now I have a hard time imagining my rolling stone settling in one spot, even on Spring Lake." Then he smiled. "Not your worry, Doc. Come out this weekend. See how far you'd have to go to restore the building and then we can talk about whether it's something you're still interested in."

Elaine felt a flutter of hope. The Bluebird was a dream she could go after. Once she'd decided to pursue something, she rarely lost. She liked her odds all of a sudden. "Fine. I'd love to visit."

"Maybe you and Dean will hit it off. Only a matter of time until you two meet anyway. Kid's always had a knack of being in the wrong place at the wrong time, which leads to stitches, splints and casts, if you know what I mean. Broke his arm when he was sixteen by falling off the roof. The girl he was trying to impress was more horrified than anything else."

Confused at the thought of anyone being foolhardy enough to climb the roof of the two-story farmhouse, Elaine opened the door and nearly shut it again at the mixture of ringing phones, arguing television pundits and the screams of an anxious child in the waiting room.

The Bluebird Bed-and-Breakfast was set in a peaceful spot overlooking Spring Lake. What she wouldn't give to spend her evenings there, catching her breath after long days of noise like this.

"Before you go, make an appointment for your six-month follow-up. Don't miss it."

She shook her finger at him. "This road trip has to come second to your health, right?"

He grumbled but the gleam in his eye was back. "And I won't forget the sunscreen."

Elaine smiled and waved goodbye. She could hear him talking with Wendy, her office manager, as she wrote her notes in his file and then asked Nina to call in refills on his medications.

"Here's the file for the next patient, Miss Hailey Dawson, age nine," Nina said as she slid over the folder. "Room two. Sneezing, cough, low fever. Looks like a cold to me—"

A loud commotion followed by the unmistakable sounds of someone vomiting in the waiting room interrupted whatever Nina was about to add to her diagnosis. Elaine had to take a deep, calming breath.

"No worries, boss. I'll take care of it." Nina patted her hand, picked up the trash can and hurried around the desk. "Oh, and your mother's already called three times this morning. The messages are on your desk." Nina paused and met her gaze. "Sorry, boss."

Elaine smiled. "No problem, Nina. I did warn you. The third divorce is almost final. Expect it to go on like this until there's a new man."

Nina saluted and disappeared into the waiting room.

For half a second, she considered checking the messages. Just because it had never been an emergency before didn't mean today was the same. Except Nina would have correctly assessed the situation just as she'd diagnosed the next patient.

Her mother could wait. Work could not.

Elaine scooped up the file and quickly entered the next exam room.

"Hailey, it's been a while since we've seen you. How's the rabbit?" Elaine shook hands with Hailey's mother, whose name she could not remember.

"He's good. Fat!" Hailey said with a delighted sparkle in her eyes just before she sneezed.

"She's got a terrible sneeze, coughs all night and I'm afraid her temperature's up," her mother said. "It's probably a cold, but I wanted to make sure."

Elaine nodded as she listened to Hailey's lungs, checked her temperature and took a look at her throat and ears. "Well, it looks to me like she's the latest to catch the cold tearing through town. Something for the cough and congestion will ease the symptoms." Elaine made some notes then ripped off the top page of her notepad and handed it to Hailey's mother. "These over-the-counter meds should help."

"So...no shot?" Hailey asked and then clapped her hands. "Yes!"

"I can tell you're disappointed. I could round up a shot for you," Elaine said. She might not have kids, but she liked them. They didn't usually return the favor, at least not while she was wearing a stethoscope around her neck.

"No, thank you," Hailey said and rolled her eyes. She straightened the bow in her curls and then carefully folded the pleats in her skirt. Hailey had a unique style. This was a girl who loved color. All of them. And all at once.

"I really like your tights, Hailey. Did you wear those to impress me?" They were striped with all the colors of the rainbow.

Elaine looked at her pale green scrubs and wished for more color of her own.

"I like rainbows. Did you know you can only see a rainbow if you're standing with your back to the sun?" Hailey nodded her head to add extra weight to her delivery. "It's true."

"Of course. Did you know that rainbows are made from light bouncing off raindrops?" Elaine answered.

Hailey rolled her eyes again, and Elaine knew she had to up her game.

"Uh, yeah. Did you know double rainbows are caused when light is reflected twice? And you can have even three or four rainbows together, although I've never seen one of those." Hailey looked a little brokenhearted at the confession.

Elaine glanced at her mother and then back to Hailey. Obviously, the girl loved science. Hailey might be Elaine a couple of decades ago.

Her mother waved a hand, a slightly rueful smile on her face. "Unless you want to do this all day, I'd move on, Dr. Watson. I keep hoping she'll grow out of it, start asking for makeup and pop music." That was another reminder of the young Elaine—a mother who wanted her to be something she wasn't.

"Maybe she'll be a doctor someday," Elaine said.

Hailey straightened her shoulders and smoothed down her skirt again. "I'm going to be the president someday."

Elaine studied her face. "Maybe you could be both."

Hailey brightened as if the idea of choosing had been a real problem. Then she sneezed, and Elaine handed her a tissue. "If you could come up with a cure for colds before you become leader of the free world, we'd all be in your debt."

Hailey held up her hand for a high five. Elaine answered Hailey's high five and watched her blow her nose. After washing her hands, Elaine opened the door. "Come in next week if the symptoms aren't significantly improved."

Hailey's mother smiled. Hailey hopped off the exam table in a blur of rainbow colors. Elaine watched them leave and then walked over to Nina. "Looks like you're right."

Elaine added a note to the file and slid it across to her.

Nina saluted and handed her the next folder. "One of the Shady Ladies is waiting. Just a follow-up for Sue Jackson."

Elaine grinned at Nina's affectionate nickname for the ladies who lived at Shady Pines, the assisted-living facility in town. If they ever heard her use it, they'd have T-shirts made up and start a bowling team to have somewhere to wear them.

"Everything okay in the waiting room?" Elaine asked as she glanced at the doorway. She did not want to check for herself.

Nina's lips twitched. "We handled it without you."

Elaine blushed and then laughed. "Of course you did. That's why I can't do this by myself."

Nina brushed that off. "Best doctor in town. Everyone says so, and you know it. Vomit being your kryptonite doesn't change that fact." She glared at the ringing phone. "Don't forget we're all headed to the Smokehouse for dinner. Wendy's birthday."

"Sorry, but I've got a shift at the clinic. You guys party without me." Elaine straightened the stack of forms on the counter in front of her and then shoved her hands into her pockets. "I'll tell Wendy happy birthday." Now that Nina had reminded her.

"Sure thing." Nina's smile didn't quite reach her eyes. "Hope you'll get a day off soon, though. It would be good for you."

Nina might be right. Elaine had been wondering if she'd know what to do with a full weekend off. She might remember to buy a birthday card for the woman who kept the lights on and the office running.

But as long as her patients needed her, she couldn't slow down.

That was what she told her mother every time the subject came up.

It wasn't entirely a lie. After a lifetime of hitting goals and pushing herself, she felt guilty if she sometimes wished for a few hours to drive to Lawrence to buy new shoes.

"Thanks for all your hard work, Nina. I couldn't manage without you." Elaine fought the urge to scurry away because a patient was waiting. She wanted to be sure Nina understood how important she was. Normally, Elaine did the job and let the emotions settle where they would, but something about today made it important to say exactly what she meant.

"You aren't dying, are you?" Nina raised both eyebrows. "You don't do the touchy-feely."

"Definitely not dying. I'm a doctor. I would know." Elaine waved her file. "And on that note, I'll get back to work."

"These sick people won't cure them-selves." Nina zoomed around her to find the next patient to fill up the currently empty exam room.

Elaine tapped the file on her hand and considered that. Nina was exactly right. She was the best doctor in town. She'd worked hard to get here, and she was doing what she was meant to do. That should be satisfying. And it was. She was proud of herself and what she'd accomplished, but lately she'd been wondering if there was supposed to be more. Or at least a bit of breathing room.

The thought of slowing down scared her. What if her practice slipped? What if she disappointed her patients?

Who would she be if she wasn't the number one doctor in town?

Elaine rubbed her forehead to ease the nagging headache that came from second-guessing her life and not getting enough sleep. Learning to relax wouldn't be the worst idea. Maybe she should take the advice she'd given Robert Collins. A new hobby could improve her whole outlook.

And if that hobby was restoring an old inn, the site of her favorite family getaways, she could also make another dream come true.

All she had to do was convince Dean Collins to hit the road again and she would have the Bluebird all for herself. How hard could it be?

CHAPTER TWO

DEAN COLLINS FOUGHT the urge to kick his feet like a bored four-year-old. After reading all the news he could get his hands on—old issues of the local paper, the state paper and his favorite online news sites—he'd come to sit on the edge of the dock while his father fished. Dean had wanted to start a conversation or make a connection or whatever the proper term was for two grown men talking about their feelings.

And they were sitting in silence.

Like they did most of the time, in fact. He raveled the edge of the latest pair of jeans he'd managed to destroy. For years, his wardrobe consisted of heavy boots, worn jeans and a collection of T-shirts that could fit in a backpack. No shorts. But these had a ripped knee and a bloodstain from an ill-fated trek from Dharamsala. That was the kind of thing he did for fun:

climb mountains and shake off a skinned knee when the climb turned into a tumble.

Now he dangled his feet in the water and hoped for a nibble—anything exciting. Adjusting to the change of pace was harder than he'd thought it would be.

"Nice weather." The whole world over, there was one topic of conversation everyone could fall back on: the weather forecast. Maybe they were on different sides of hot vs. cold or wet vs. dry, but everyone had an opinion about the weather. Tall Pines was no exception.

In fact, the weekly forecast enjoyed some prime real estate on the last page of the *Times*. Most of the world had gone to infographics. Not so here. He'd actually had to read the forecast so he was prepared to converse.

Obviously, there was no need yet. His father's grunt could be taken as either agreement or disagreement, but it didn't do much to pick up the conversational ball and run with it.

Even if they'd had a rousing conversation about precipitation, he'd still be bored.

Or maybe restless, antsy. Thinking could

be trouble, but the urge to move usually kept him distracted. Outrunning bad memories was a habit he'd picked up early. His problem now was that, no matter how fast or far he went, they were catching up.

So, with his first strategy failing, he'd come back to the place it all started: home.

"How'd the doctor visit go?" A question that required either an answer or outright rudeness. That ought to open the door.

"Good."

So the question wasn't as foolproof as he thought. "Sheesh, no need to talk my ear off."

His dad glanced in his direction. "You're one to talk. Ready to tell me about this concussion and why you don't sleep?"

Dean pulled his feet out of the water and stood. "You know the military. Bunch of worriers."

His dad's lips formed a thin line, and Dean was afraid he was coming up with questions Dean had no answers for. "Right. They do love to coddle the journalists they cram in beside their delicate soldiers."

Dean rolled up the sleeves of the flannel shirt he'd pulled on over his ragged jeans and stepped into flip-flops that looked as though they'd been feeding a small family of rodents. "The unit I was with got caught in a firefight with a small band of rebels. There was an explosion. No one was killed, but I hit my head. Saw stars. That was enough for the army doctors." He shoved his hands into his pockets. "You know me. I've had way worse."

His dad was quiet for too long. Finally, he said, "At least it brought you home for a few days."

His father never had been good at guilt trips, but he might be getting better.

"I'm glad you had a nice visit," Dean mumbled and turned to go…somewhere. He had no idea where, but he'd made his effort for the day.

His father's voice stopped him. "Invited her out. She's coming to take a look around."

"Who? The doctor? Why?" The place definitely would not show well, not yet. He'd get to work on that soon, but not today. Today was for forcing himself to take it slow. He had to learn sometime, and the sooner, the better.

His dad sighed and pulled his pole out of the water to set it on the dock. "She used to visit. Loved the tearoom and the inn."

Dean looked over his shoulder at the house he'd grown up in. When his mother was alive, she'd settled for nothing less than pristine white paint with bright blue shutters, precisely manicured gardens and flags snapping in the breeze to welcome visitors.

The gray boards and peeling paint, ragged flower beds and air of general fatigue almost made it hard to believe it was the same place.

Except the beautiful bones were still there. He counted six windows across the front of the house, the finest guest rooms, and wished he'd thought to camp in one of those. The view of the lake might have helped calm some of his anger and irritation and just…overwhelming emotion.

Something had to or he might have a meltdown, lose the control he'd worked so hard to hold on to. Sometimes, when he was staring out the window in the middle of the night, he wondered if he was already there.

"Hope she's not too disappointed," his

father murmured, and Dean turned to see his dad's eyes were locked on him.

"I wish I'd known, Dad. I might have been able to help." And the guilt he'd been buried under when he'd lurched to a stop under the old oak tree would have been much lighter. But he hadn't known. Because he hadn't been home in a long time.

Without his mother to hold them together, he and his dad had struggled. It was easier to take the next story, jump on a plane and tell himself it was all for his career. His father never complained about missing him and never mentioned needing help. He'd thought they were both satisfied.

Until that career nearly killed him, and he had nowhere else to go.

"Well, I'm here now, and I think I know what to do to get this place up and running. We're going to make some changes." He tried to infuse the statement with confidence. The last time he'd suggested changes, he'd been too young and unstable to convince his father. Now both of them and the Bluebird were in desperate need of a change.

"About that…" His father turned to look

out over the shore next to the short dock. "She wants to buy the Bluebird. Renovate it. Maybe we should consider that. Neither one of us should be tied down by the past."

Speechless, Dean stared at his pale feet and the weathered boards of the dock. He'd never really thought about a life without the inn. Knowing it would always be here when he was ready made it easier to brave the most dangerous spots on the planet. He'd trusted his father to make sure he had a home just in case he ever needed somewhere safe.

Getting the Bluebird open would be hard work, but running a fish camp like he had in mind or even a country inn seemed like a vacation after dodging bullets and crooked foreign politicians for years.

That career, the one he'd loved for so long, wasn't a smart way to spend the rest of what would be too short a life. If he could learn to slow down, settle in, everything would be perfect. If he couldn't do that in Tall Pines, he had no idea where to go next.

Maybe it was time to have the conversation he'd been putting off since he arrived.

"Listen, Dad," Dean said as he scrubbed his hands through his hair, "you probably have some doubts, but I have a good plan, one that will work. You'll still be free to fish or hit the road or whatever. You can trust everything to me."

His dad was silent, and Dean fought the urge to explain himself to this quiet man who'd always been content like this, sitting on the dock and watching the water. This plan to explore the country all alone was a new development, another one Dean was having a hard time adjusting to. He watched his dad stand easily and bend down to grasp the fishing pole.

"For how long?" His father spoke softly, but it was a loud thought in the silence of Spring Lake on a summer day.

That was the only question he didn't have an answer for, and it was the most important one.

"Maybe you could explain what's going on, son." His father reached up to squeeze his shoulder, the same way he'd done when Dean was a teenager and needed encouragement. It wasn't one of his mother's perfumed hugs, but the way he wanted to fling his arms around his father's neck was just… He was a grown man. Crazy enough to travel the world with a camera and a backpack. He could handle his own problems.

"I think…" How could he say it without alarming his father? The last thing he wanted, now that his dad was considering moving forward, was to hold him back. "You know how, when you're busy, you keep adding things on, piling on one more job and hurrying through this thing to get to the next until finally something happens and you can't catch up anymore?"

His father frowned and considered the weathered boards under his feet. "Been a long time, but maybe. That what happened to you? Need a vacation? You could always hit the road with me. Sure would be exciting."

Dean gave a hard laugh. Yeah, that was what happened. Except it was so much worse than missing deadlines or being late with bills. Watching men fight for their lives took a toll. Sitting on a beach and soaking up the sun was only the first step in his recovery, but it was one he could take immediately.

"I need a new life. I need to sleep without the threat of death or the memory of my last assignment waking me up. I need…" Dean hated even saying the words out loud, admitting his weakness, especially to his father. "If I don't do something new, I'm afraid I'm not going to make it, Dad."

His father didn't look away until Dean awkwardly cleared his throat. These attacks of emotion that came out of nowhere rattled Dean, but the truth was he had no control over them. He hated that.

They might shock his father, but he'd never let Dean down, either.

"And you think this place can give you what you need?" The doubt in his voice was clear. Dean tried not to take it personally, because he wasn't fully convinced himself.

They both heard the crunch of gravel down the washed-out road.

"Guess she's here." His father squeezed his shoulder again. "We'll figure it out, son." Dean hoped to convince them both that letting him have the Bluebird was the best decision, but the right words wouldn't come.

"Just meet her. I'll show her how run-down the inn is. Might be enough to convince her she'd like to build her own house somewhere nearby. We could be neighbors, and everyone's happy." His father didn't look like he believed that, though.

"Hard to imagine another space like this anywhere, Dad." Dean was relieved to be on firmer emotional footing. His father whistled as they walked up the hill to the overgrown yard.

When the car door shut on a sensible gray four-door sedan, Dean watched the doctor, if she was a doctor, tiptoe carefully through the gravel in sandals that had no business outside the city streets. Instead of scrubs or a white coat, she was wearing a sundress. She looked like a model for a beachside getaway. Obviously, she'd dressed for the old Bluebird Bed-and-Breakfast. If she'd known about today's disaster, she'd be wearing work boots or mourning. Either way, she was not prepared for what she was about to see.

Didn't mean she wasn't pretty in a very

serious, very studious kind of way. Her dark glasses perched on the end of her nose, and her hair was twisted up on top of her head. Except for the setting, she could be out for brunch with the ladies.

"Hi. I hope I'm not late, Mr. Collins," she said breathlessly as she stepped into the grass in front of the porch. "Beautiful day for a drive."

"Shoulda warned you about the road. You could have called me from the highway to save your car a little wear and tear." His father propped his hands on his hips. Dean had seen the pose a few hundred times. It was the one his father struck when he was carefully assessing the situation.

"Oh, it's not so bad." She held out her hand. "I'm Elaine, Dr. Watson. It's nice to meet you, Dean."

Caught off guard, Dean grasped her hand in his. She surprised him again when she gave it a firm shake and then dropped it as though it was too hot to hold.

"What do you think?" his father asked. "Not quite what you remembered, is it?" The uncertainty on his father's face had a few defensive comments popping to mind, but before Dean could get any of them ready to fire, she said, "I love it."

She slowly stepped forward as if she was drawn toward the building, being towed in by a mixture of old memories and the charm of the faded wraparound porch.

"I can't believe it's taken this long to come back," Elaine said quietly. "Only good manners have kept me from showing up on your doorstep, Mr. Collins."

His father laughed. "And crazy hours, double shifts and patients who need you have no doubt hampered your ability to explore." She smiled at his father over her shoulder and instead of being the enemy out to build a better offer than anything he could put together, she was a beautiful woman. A beautiful, happy woman in a breezy sundress posed in front of the old farmhouse as though she was a model spokesperson to sell relaxing vacations. She seemed to fit the landscape perfectly and at the same time made him wonder what it would be like to be the man who put the smile on her face.

That smile was dangerous. Land-mine dangerous.

Determined to get things back on track, and Dr. Elaine Watson chugging down the washed-out road as quickly as possible, Dean roughly cleared his throat. "Well, you're here now. Might as well get the whole tired picture."

When she turned her eyes to him, he was thankful for the glass lenses, which were probably the only things saving him from incineration. She didn't miss a thing, and as she assessed him from head to toe, he was aware again that he'd dressed as if his only choices were in the Lost and Found. "Sorry. If I'd known we were having company, I'd have put on my dress flip-flops."

Dr. Watson didn't like him, didn't want to like him, and the sharp eyes of a competitor were easy to see. She was here to win. When his father frowned at him, Dean almost apologized, but then her cool smile made him double down. She obviously had her act together while everything about him was scattered across the globe. She could put up with ratty flip-flops for a few minutes.

But her charmed smile and the way his father stepped up to offer her his arm made it crystal clear how weak his own position was. He followed them up the steps and watched the doctor spin around to take in the view, the best part of the Bluebird Bed-and-Breakfast. The inn was situated on a peaceful cove of Spring Lake, so there wasn't much traffic close to the shore. It felt like the three of them were the only people on the planet. The falling-down boat slips ruined the view a little, but he could picture them the way his mother had insisted: clean with fresh paint, a shiny red metal roof on top and an American flag blowing in the breeze.

Since his plan was to run the whole place as a fishing camp, restoring the docks and adding a small marina store would be his first project. Fishermen didn't really need fresh paint or new carpet, but they had to have a spot to keep the boat.

"I could stay right here all day," Elaine said and stretched her arms out wide.

"Not much excitement compared to your waiting room or the emergency clinic," his father answered.

"That's why I need it." Elaine glanced at Dean and then quickly looked away, probably to see if he understood her motivation. He did. But she and her…neatness were annoying.

He propped his hands on his hips and studied the view. Somehow the restlessness eased while he was standing here, looking past the overgrown yard to the calm waters of Spring Lake. Had to be the setting. The company was not soothing at all. Maybe the magic of home was finally starting to work.

"Let's see the inside," Elaine said and towed his father to the ancient screen door. The paint, which had once been a bright blue, was peeling, but it could be restored easily. That door fit the character of the Bluebird perfectly even if the pop as it slammed shut could make him jerk as if he'd heard a gunshot.

His father opened the door, and they stepped inside. The view was not inspiring. Dry, scratched hardwoods that had gleamed like mirrors when his mother ran the place, wallpaper that was in excellent shape if twenty years out of date and dust-covered furniture. His father used only the living quarters upstairs, so the bottom floor was frozen in time. Preserved, but not alive.

Except for the kitchen.

As he trailed the exploration party, he heard Elaine say, "Well, it looks like it could use some updating. Do all the appliances work?"

He'd had the same question. As far as he could tell, his father lived on cereal and sandwiches. As long as the refrigerator was running, he was set. The fact that she didn't make a big deal out of the biggest deal said something about how Dr. Watson played the game.

"Yep, stove, fridge, whatever's here works." His dad ran a hand through his hair as if he wasn't quite sure how to address the most obvious problem in the room. "And all the cabinets...well..."

There wasn't much to say about that. The fact that they were all missing made it clear what he was talking about.

"I decided it was silly to have the old Bluebird sitting empty, but I knew reopening was going to take some renovation." His dad shrugged.

"So you started with the kitchen." Elaine

nodded as if she approved. "And are you going to—" she waved a hand vaguely "—finish?"

"Nah, I remembered why I hadn't taken on any DIY projects in twenty-plus years." His father opened the refrigerator door to show the good doctor that it was fully functional.

When Elaine glanced at him for help, Dean had to shrug his shoulders. It didn't make a lot of sense to him, either, but he'd had some time for the state of the kitchen to sink in.

"Why is that, Mr. Collins?" She tilted her head to the side as if she was so very curious about why anyone would leave a kitchen torn up like this one. It was a valid question.

"I hate DIY projects." His father grimaced. "That's why I didn't do them when Martha was alive and why I had no problem letting everything ride after she died. Eventually, even the regulars started staying at the chain hotel in Lawrence." He toed the peeling linoleum. "I purely hate construction of any kind. Been running the place so long, it was nice to have a vacation. All that money we saved for someday, when we could retire to see the world, kept the lights on. And I'd rather fish. So I did."

"Because you could," Dean added. "I don't blame you a bit. And you should say that Mom wouldn't *let* you tackle any home improvements."

Then he leaned closer to the doctor. "Very bad for his blood pressure and hers, if I recall correctly." He was irritated she didn't at least smile in return. He hadn't spent a lot of time charming women lately, but surely he hadn't completely lost his touch. If she liked him, maybe she'd back off, drop her offer.

Her small frown was cuter than it should be. Dr. Elaine Watson was obviously conscientious if a mention of his dad's blood pressure could concern her even on her days off.

"Do you still have the cabinets?" she asked as she turned away from Dean. "Maybe I could get someone to put them back in." The look she shot him suggested that maybe he should have already taken care of it. Dean considered his father and wondered if there was more to the story than he knew. Why was she giving him a glare that said, "Why aren't you ashamed of yourself?"

"Hey, I'm not all that handy myself," Dean said with a laugh. "That must be genetic, but we could hire someone to put the cabinets in. I'm sure they're exactly what I need when I open the Tall Pines Fish Camp."

"Fish camp?" Elaine wrinkled her nose as if she could already pick up a whiff of lake water and fish scales. "What a waste of this space."

Annoyed again, Dean sent a pointed look around the gutted kitchen. "Or maybe exactly the right solution. Fishermen don't need granite countertops. I could have this place up and running in no time."

Elaine's snort stopped him in his tracks. His father tried to hide a grin behind a cough. "Did I say something funny?"

"I'm sure they're going to love the antiques in the front room and the morning-glory wallpaper that covers your entry."

Morning glories. Finally! He'd been racking his brain to try to remember what the blue flowers were. His mother had loved them and babied a couple of vines in her garden. He wondered if they'd survived the neglect.

Dean was determined to ignore the doctor's very good point. He would have to get a bigger television and some comfortable chairs. If he recalled correctly, most of the furniture in the front room looked like reproductions from an era when people were smaller and chair legs could be much fussier.

"Maybe the kitchen would work for your fish camp," she said with a grimace, "but I bet I could open before you would."

"Really." He didn't believe her for a minute. She was a doctor. He doubted she'd ever swung a hammer in her life. He was unemployed, with all the time in the world. Demolition might be his only contribution, but he wasn't afraid of hard physical work. There was no question as to who would win this race.

"When I want something badly, I don't waste time. You'd be shocked how quickly I could get this building restored and open for business." One corner of her mouth turned up, and if he wasn't mistaken, that was the fire of determination in her eyes. "Bet on it."

He crossed his arms over his chest. "I don't have to. This is my home. My father's already promised to let me give it a shot. I'm going to make my changes on my own timeline. You lose."

Her lips tightened, and she closed her eyes for two seconds. "Of course. You're right. I'd forgotten in the excitement of seeing the Bluebird." She stepped back. "Thank you for the tour, Mr. Collins." She held out her hand. Dean reluctantly shook it. Surely it couldn't be that simple. Then she smiled at his father. "When this fails, Mr. Collins, please give me a shot. As long as the building's still standing, I'm interested in having my chance."

Dean held up one hand. "*When* it fails?"

"Of course, I should have said *if*," Elaine replied, but the look on her face didn't seem to match her words. She wasn't going to back down.

"Explain to me why I'm going to fail," Dean answered.

"Well, one look at you says you're not big on...planning ahead." Her frosty gaze might have raised goose bumps if it hadn't been a lovely summer day. "A renovation like this requires planning, marketing, new staff. You're going to need money. Do you even have a business plan?"

Her doubts were clear. The fact was he didn't have a plan. But he'd need one. He had some savings, but getting his camp set up would take a lot of cash. A new marina wouldn't be cheap. Mortgaging his home to finance a gamble without a detailed schedule and some consideration of how he might cover the payments was crazy. His confidence took a hit, but the only way to deal with a situation like this was to pretend everything was under control.

Convincing his dad he could handle the details was critical.

"And you're interested in having your chance for what? To move into an inn with eight guest rooms…all by yourself." He didn't have to ask about a husband or kids. No ring. No doubt she was focusing on her career. "Kind of a big house for a single woman. All alone. Out here by yourself with the wildlife."

Elaine opened her mouth and then closed

it. She raised one finger. "I'm only going to say this because…" Her lips tightened to swallow whatever it was she planned to add. "Never mind. Doesn't matter."

She headed for the entryway. "Mr. Collins, I hope this works out, for your sake."

"Everybody just…wait." His father's voice was loud, and Dean could hear the anger bubbling under the surface. He wasn't sure Elaine was going to stop, but she jerked to a halt next to the door.

"Before this goes too far, I've got something to say." His dad narrowed his eyes, and Dean got the impression that he'd better keep his mouth zipped until his dad was done.

"Dean, you're my son. I want you to have this place if it will…I don't know, make you happy. But," he said as he held up a hand, "this woman saved my life. And she loves the place."

"Saved your life?" Dean said as he rubbed his forehead. "What does that mean?"

"I only did my job," Elaine said and crossed her arms. "Any other doctor would have done the same."

"Somebody tell me what we're talking about." Dean propped his hands on his hips. "Now."

The sudden tightness in his chest made it hard to breathe.

Elaine's eyebrows rose, and Dean got the impression there was only one thing she was interested in telling him, and that was exactly where to get off.

"I went into the emergency clinic with chest pains. That's all. I'm fine." His father tried a reassuring smile, but it looked so wrong on him that Dean said, "No way. You didn't tell me any of this. When?" He turned to the doctor because he was certain he stood a better chance of getting a straight answer from her.

"It's been almost two years. He's done great since then. Takes his meds. Lost some weight." She shrugged. "And he's making a change for the better with this new plan to hit the road. He's a model patient, actually. That's rare."

"We don't have to talk about this now. Let's come up with some suggestions on what to do here." His father paced in a small circle on the dull hardwoods.

He and Elaine stared at each other for a long second, and he wondered if she felt the same tension he did. When her cheeks turned a pale pink and she looked away, he thought maybe she did.

"How about a real bet?" His father paused. "I'll hit the road. You'll both have time to make plans, figure out the money and talk to the bank. I'll listen to both proposals and decide based on what's best for the Bluebird. A month? How's that?"

Elaine looked as if she was about to argue. He could almost see the dueling urges on her face. She wanted the Bluebird, but she needed to do the right thing. He waited to see which would win.

And he braced himself when she stepped up next to him.

"It's a bet." She held out her hand.

"I love a challenge," Dean said as he gripped her hand, surprised again at the warmth that spread from her to him. "This could be what I was looking for."

"I guess we'll see." The smile was back. A simple curve of her lips that gave her eyes a sparkle. The way Dean's world shifted in that second worried him. He'd started the game. He had no choice but to win. Unless the Bluebird worked its magic, he was lost.

ELAINE TRIED TO understand the emotion in Dean's eyes. For a split second she'd thought it was fear or maybe worry, but that didn't make any sense. He was a guy who traveled the world, photographed wars and looked supremely confident in ratty clothes. On top of that, he was family. If anyone was a solid contender, it was him. Had her certainty that the fish camp was a bad idea convinced him to reconsider his plans?

"Well," Robert said, looking from her to Dean and back, "good. That's settled. Got an appointment with a contractor tomorrow. Here's what we'll do. Get him to take a look, maybe give you estimates on what you'd like to renovate."

Elaine refused to take a step back even though she was closer to Dean Collins than she was strictly comfortable with. She could see he had hazel eyes, a mix of brown and green that was warm and possibly too intelligent for an easy win. Getting this close to him was a bad idea for a long list of reasons. Still, she was not going to back down. Not now. He'd made his opinion of her clear. He thought she was a fragile flower. He was wrong.

When Robert coughed quietly, she and Dean both turned.

"How will you decide a winner?" Elaine asked.

Dean's snort set her teeth on edge, and she did her best to forget her own snort of disbelief earlier. Maybe turnabout snorting was fair play.

She and Dean watched Robert think. He paced. He cracked his knuckles. He opened his mouth and changed his mind twice.

Then he said, "We'll get judges. That's the fairest thing. All three of us. That way, an impartial panel will decide what's best for the Bluebird and for Tall Pines."

"And you don't have to disappoint either one of us." Elaine raised her eyebrows.

"Why, I never thought of that," Robert said and smiled. "Excellent point, Doc. I like this plan. What do you think?"

Dean ran his hands through messy, dark curls that were entirely too long. Men should not have such nice hair. It was unfair. Of course, he looked as if he'd combed it with a pasta fork.

"Fine with me." Dean's gaze locked with hers, and she experienced again the breathless awareness she'd felt when she stepped out of her car to see him there, a part of her favorite view in the world.

She wouldn't let it rattle her.

She was going to give this her best shot. After all, she'd played to win her whole life. Even though she'd built the busiest medical practice in the area, she needed to strengthen her position. The judges would have a hard time choosing her over Dean, Robert's son and a hometown boy. She raised her chin and nodded. "Me, too, but I think I should move in while I'm planning."

Dean shook his head while Robert smiled broadly. "Great idea. Give you a real good feel for what it'll take to put it back together."

They both turned to Dean. He waved his hands in surrender. "Fine. Plenty of space. Just don't expect room service."

Robert clapped his hands once loudly.

"Good. Let's get this show on the road. Pack a bag. Move in. Meet with the contractor tomorrow if you've got time." He put one hand on the small of her back and started to escort her onto the porch. Elaine managed to keep the satisfied smile from creeping through.

"If you don't mind, Dad, I'd like to talk with Dr. Watson." Dean followed them out. "Alone."

Robert responded eloquently without saying a word. There was a threat in his eyes. Dean had better be on his best behavior.

Elaine had to fight the smile that came with the shot of pleasure that someone was looking out for her. Dean raised his hands in surrender, and Robert disappeared inside.

"I'm not sure you'll have as much privacy as you want, but feel free to say whatever it is that's bothering you, Mr. Collins." She adjusted her purse strap and studied the view carefully. This would be no harder than talking to any other upset family member. Doctors spent a lot of time delivering bad news and listening to complaints.

Dean checked inside the shadowed foyer. "You could be right. Two things." He held up two fingers, probably so he wouldn't lose his spot in the conversation.

At the unkind thought, Elaine knew she had to take her competitiveness down a notch. There was no need to get nasty. Ever.

Even if she knew how to.

"Call me Dean. Call him Robert. Otherwise, this whole thing is going to get weird," Dean said as he eased into a creaky rocking chair and motioned her to the other one.

She studied the peeling paint before she sat. "Fine. And?"

"Tell me why this means so much to you."

She tilted her head, hoping he could read what she thought about his tone.

"Fine. Please. I want to understand." He eased the rocking chair into motion, and the rhythmic creak combined with the cool shade and the stillness of the lake made it easy to answer his question, if only to sit there a few minutes longer.

"The last time I visited, I was twelve. Like most twelve-year-old girls, I wished things were different. My mother wanted me to wear my hair down and try makeup, and my dad wanted me to keep my mother happy while he did his own thing. But Mom loved this place, and she loved drinking tea on this porch. And your mother was so kind that we all somehow got along when we were here." Elaine started rocking back and forth, too, her creaks a perfect counterpoint to his. "Then my parents divorced. Loudly. We never came back to the Bluebird or Tall Pines."

Dean contemplated the shoreline. "So it's got some good memories. I can understand that. Is that enough reason to spend this much time and money? Maybe the money doesn't matter to someone like you. Couldn't you make nice memories somewhere else?"

"Couldn't you?" Elaine asked. "No, of course not. They're memories, Dean. Nothing is the same now. My father is happily remarried with a nice wife and a new family. And my mother is...well, she's not as settled. These are the memories I want to keep."

"At the expense of mine?" He didn't look at her, and it was a good thing.

This was the troublesome point—the idea that she would cause Robert any pain by getting what she wanted. If Dean and Robert were strangers, she'd get the Bluebird. There was no question in her mind. This concern for Robert hampered her efforts.

Now that she knew his father had kept his health problems a secret, she was more forgiving of Dean's time away. Exciting careers could take over a life easily. Being a doctor didn't often involve the risks he took, but the adrenaline rush could be intense.

"It seems you've done fine through the years with the memories alone. Why is now any different?" Maybe she couldn't go for the kill. That didn't mean she had to give in.

"It just is. Now is different. I'm different. And it matters." Dean stood and waited for her to get the picture that this conversation was over.

"Are you sure you can abide by this competition?" Elaine asked as she slowly walked down the steps toward her car. "Tell me here and now, before I pack my bags and drive down that road again. I'll back down before I cause your father any pain."

"But it will kill you to throw in the towel before anyone rings the bell." Dean glanced toward the foyer and nodded. "Yes, to prove to my father that I have what it takes, including the commitment to stick this out, I will agree to the bet and the rules, but I intend to win."

CHAPTER THREE

DEAN STEPPED INSIDE and shut the door, snapping Elaine out of her reverie. "Rude," she muttered and got into her car.

She made her way to the highway. In the middle of making a mental list of the things she'd have to pack, her phone rang, and she hit the hands-free button to talk. "Hi, Mom." She didn't even have to look. It had to be her mother.

"I haven't heard from you in a while, so I thought I'd make sure you're okay."

A while meaning approximately two hours. Checking to make sure she was okay was more about her mother not being okay. "I'm fine. What's up?"

"Oh, not much. I started thinking about the reception we had and how you and Jerry argued about the proper way to serve red wine. Remember, he was certain it had to be warm, and you said to chill the wine and warm it in the hand? What an impression you must have made on your new stepfather. I thought that was the craziest thing to argue about." Her voice broke on the last word. "You're so much like your father sometimes. So smart. Even when you were a little girl, I'd listen to the two of you talk and just…marvel."

Elaine couldn't recall the wine conversation. She and her mother's last husband, Jerry, had often agreed to disagree, but she'd never intended to cause friction in any of her mother's marriages.

Being compared to her father didn't surprise her at all.

Elaine could remember the days when she'd hoped to be exactly like her father.

Now she was afraid that her wish had come true. He lived to work. Most days, she did, too.

"Mom, are you drinking wine by any chance?" Elaine parked in front of a small line of apartments. She'd lived here since she'd come to Tall Pines to satisfy the terms of the scholarship that had helped her get through medical school debt free.

"Yes."

The hiccup made Elaine smile as she switched the call to her phone. She unlocked the door and asked, "How much?"

"It's my…second glass." Her mother's answer was a relief. Maybe she was too emotional, but she'd never been a big drinker. Elaine could picture her mother perched on the end of her expensive couch, not a single hair of her carefully highlighted bob out of order. Even tipsy, she'd be well behaved and beautiful.

Sometimes Elaine wondered if she was the only person who saw the emotional, messy, ragged side of Catherine Stillman. She was the model hostess with lovely manners, but inside, her mother still seemed to be searching for something.

Elaine, on the other hand, always looked a bit frazzled. Her sundress was wrinkled after less than three hours, and the curls escaping her careful updo were driving her crazy. Scrubs and a ponytail fit her better.

And if she was searching for anything, it was the way things used to be.

"You know you're going to be happy again, right? Have you thought about taking a class like we talked about?" Elaine pulled a bag out of her closet and started shoving clothes inside.

While she packed, she thought about all the activities her mother should consider instead of focusing on how she didn't have a husband anymore. A part-time job, a class at the community college, a new hobby or a trip to someplace she'd always dreamed of. They were all reasonable, fun options. If Elaine's schedule ever cleared up, she might give something on the list a try herself. As always, her mother had one answer. "I don't want to do that by myself."

"Mom, do you remember the Bluebird Bed-and-Breakfast? The inn we used to visit here in Tall Pines?" Elaine crossed her fingers and hoped this didn't lead to a meltdown.

"Sure, that pretty old farmhouse on the lake. Had the tastiest sugar cookies as I recall." Her mother paused as she sipped her wine. "Your father fished, and we ruled the world from that shady porch. Those were nice times. Before your father ruined it all."

Elaine took a deep breath. This was the tricky part. Any time her father came up in conversation, things could get out of control fast. "Yeah, so the owner is a patient. I took a trip out there today because he's considering selling."

"But you're a doctor. What would you do with an inn? The last thing you need is another job. No, you should spend fewer hours working." Her mother left off the advice to get married, have kids, probably because she didn't want an argument, either.

"Maybe we could reopen it. Together. What would you think about that?" She held her breath while she waited for the answer.

"I'm not sure, Elaine. I mean, the memories…"

Her mother hadn't said no. That was a new development. "It could be fun, but it may not work out anyway, so you've got time to consider it."

"I will. I promise," her mother said quietly. "Thanks for talking, Elaine. I swear, no more men. Ever. This time is different."

Right. Elaine was sure she'd heard that the last time, too. And with the boyfriends in between, one of whom had been so steady and good for her mother she'd mourned him like…well, her own father.

Her father wasn't dead. He was just gone, content with his new wife and two sons.

Neither of whom were doctors.

Not yet anyway. There was still time, and her youngest brother did mention medical school now and then.

At least her mother's wails had already quieted to grumbles. This seemed to indicate she was on the mend. The fact that she'd gotten there quicker than Elaine expected was a positive sign. There'd been surprisingly few bitter warnings about men or guilt trips about grandkids. Elaine was tired of hearing that all her mother's problems would be solved if Elaine would just get married and have babies. Following her mother's train of thought could be exhausting.

She'd had plenty of time to build up her endurance. When her father left, Elaine had picked up the pieces. Ever since, she'd hung on to the roller-coaster ride that was her mother. Relationships came and went, men were magic until they disappointed her and then Elaine was a lifeline.

She was used to the pattern by now, even if she tried to alter it.

Her mother was only three hours away, but Elaine was always working. When things were good, the distance was easy. Her mother's happy phone conversations satisfied them both. When her mother was going through a breakup, the distance could be a relief.

"You aren't planning to drive anywhere, are you, Mom?"

This time her mother gave a disbelieving grunt. "Do you think I'm crazy? I'm going to take a nap."

"Sounds good. Call me tomorrow." After her mother mumbled goodbye, Elaine tossed her phone on the couch cushion next to her purse, dropped down beside it and covered her eyes with both hands.

Taking a day off and doing anything other than laundry and napping was rare, but she was glad she'd made the trip out to see the Bluebird. If only Dean Collins wasn't going to be such a problem. She had a small chance to beat him. Ignoring him was going to be a lot harder.

But leaving this economy apartment would be no problem. There were no pictures on the wall, and the only decoration she'd added was three small framed photos of her with her parents, all taken at award ceremonies. The furniture belonged to her landlord, Edna. Why she hadn't done more to make the apartment feel like home was something she should consider long and hard. Some other time.

Today she was going to grab her bag, go back and move right in. She'd start leaving her stamp as soon as possible.

Men would come and go and take her mother's sanity with them, but the Bluebird would last. Getting attached to the place that held such sweet memories only made sense.

"Hit the road, Elaine. There'll be plenty of time to figure out the cure for your problems on that beautiful porch."

She smiled at the idea and did her best to ignore the fact that she was talking to herself.

After one more quick trip through the closet and tiny bathroom, Elaine had enough necessities to get her through a week or so. She grabbed her bag and purse and locked up.

On her way to the Bluebird, she decided

to take advantage of the rare combination of a beautiful day and free time, so she drove around the town square. Elaine was happy to see the tourists. Tall Pines was her new home, and almost everyone here depended on these visitors. Spring could be hit and miss, but now that the trees were blooming and temperatures were inching back up, shoppers wandered down the streets, bags in hand.

As a child, she'd loved every single one of these shops.

She stopped at a crosswalk and watched a boy who kept a serious stare locked on her car as he walked by, one hand grasped by his mother.

A few minutes later, as she headed down the rutted road toward the Bluebird, Elaine wondered whether reopening the inn could help draw even more tourists to her adopted hometown.

She parked next to a dilapidated Jeep that had to belong to Dean Collins. It matched his wardrobe perfectly.

She grabbed her bag and thought about honking the horn, just to let him know she was back and ready to get started. The kitchen was appalling, every room required work and the whole farmhouse needed a coat of paint, but the potential was all there.

Elaine was hit by an unexpected wave of excitement. The renovation would be expensive and a lot of hard work, but the reward, a home that connected her to some of the happiest times in her life, was worth it. She couldn't remember wanting anything as much as she wanted this.

In only one day, she'd pinned her hopes on a long shot.

Okay, Elaine, too emotional. Take a deep breath.

She did. Then she got out of the car like a totally rational person and almost made it to the steps when she could feel someone watching her. Dean was near the dock again. Deciding that she should begin as she meant to go on, she marched down to meet him.

"I'm back." *What a terrible opening line, Dr. Obvious.* "Which room should I take?"

He waved his filleting knife, and they both watched a bit of…fillet plop into the water. Dean studied her face, waiting for a reaction. She stepped closer. "Hmm, you'd never make it as a surgeon."

Then she raised her eyebrows at him. She was a doctor. A little bit of gore had no effect on her.

"Take any guest room you want. They're all the same. Dusty. Stuck in the past."

She nodded. "Okay. Thank goodness that's easy enough to change." Pleased with that parting line, she spun on one heel and bit back a curse as she nearly toppled right off the dock. Determined not to look at him, she pretended she was absorbed by the beauty of the inn. And she was, even if it was hard to see.

For the first time in a while, taking a break from the emergency clinic seemed like a good plan. She could weed the garden, try to rescue Martha Collins's roses.

Before she went inside, she paused to look at the bluebird boxes on the hill. She couldn't see any birds, but she remembered how much she'd loved to wait for them. Before the trips to the inn, she'd never seen a bluebird, so every single sighting had added to the magic of Spring Lake. Her parents got along here. Her mother smiled, and her father laughed.

Even then she'd been more scientist than fairy-tale princess, but the bluebirds seemed to promise happy endings. The nesting boxes had faded like the rest of the place. She should research how to fix them up. The Bluebird Bed-and-Breakfast needed bluebirds.

CHAPTER FOUR

AFTER A LONG, sleepless night, Dean slipped out the front door and headed to the dock. The sun was rising over the lake. Watching the light spread across the calm surface was the only compensation for being unable to close his eyes without nightmares shaking him awake. A week of peaceful mornings like this had started to work a little of the familiar magic.

He cast his line and pretended to fish. If his father saw him, maybe he'd see it as a sign of progress. And maybe he'd decide to join him.

Steady, quick footfalls distracted him from his accidental meditation. He looked over his shoulder and winced at the morning stiffness of his old injuries, large and small. Elaine Watson didn't even glance his direction as she ran by.

Joggers usually seemed to be suffering,

but Elaine's face was as calm as his own. And she was fast.

Of course she was. He had a feeling if she committed to something, she did it well. She probably ran because it was good exercise, but she excelled at it because she saw no other option.

"Must be exhausting." He'd never aspired to be the best. Adventure and the chance to make a difference had been enough to keep him going. For a long time anyway.

Anyone who became a doctor had to have that same desire to help, didn't she?

Dean's shoulders slumped as he turned back to the water and closed his eyes. He didn't really want to have anything in common with Elaine Watson.

"Jogging? Probably is exhausting." His father held out a mug and sat next to him. "Guess it doesn't matter if you enjoy it."

Dean sipped his hot black coffee and felt the satisfaction spread all the way to his bones. "Thanks, Dad. This hits the spot."

"Don't tell the doctor. Little bit of caffeine's good for the soul, I'm convinced." His father cast his line, and neither one of them said anything for the longest time.

The fish weren't biting. Everything was quiet.

His father's silence matched Dean's mood. The tense restlessness was missing, and Dean appreciated the break. They were both content to sit there, staring out across the lake. He lost track of how long he waited for a bite.

"I've missed this," Dean said. "Peace. Quiet." He lifted his fishing rod and reeled in his useless bait. He might do better with a new lure, but that would require effort. This morning was nearly flawless as it was. He shifted, cast his line again and ignored the mental picture of Elaine's disapproving stare.

"No one trying to shoot you with a long-range scope. No threats of drinking bad water or falling off a mountain." His dad sighed. "It's the little things."

Dean's rusty laugh was loud in the still morning. "Yeah, I guess so."

"If your mother was around, she'd already have us jumping, ticking off the to-do list." The click of his father's reel was comforting, a sound that would always remind him of home.

"I expected the doctor to have already sounded an alarm, mustered the troops and conquered something." Dean checked his watch, the one he could dump now that he was back in Tall Pines. Everything moved at its own pace in this town. "I mean, it's almost eight. Daylight's wasting."

His father nodded. "You could both stand to do a better job at relaxing."

"*I* am sitting at the end of a dock, not catching fish. It doesn't get any more relaxed than this." Dean shifted his pole and watched the ripples in the water.

"Sure. After staring out the window all night long. I bet that's pretty relaxing, too." His dad didn't look at him when he added, "We have a doctor in the house. She might be able to help."

"I don't need any help," Dean snapped. "I'm fine."

How did his father know about his long nights? Dean stood up so quickly he had to take a step back from the edge of the dock or risk landing in the lake. Another surge of those ridiculous emotions, this time anger. He had to get a grip.

"Sorry, Dad. I appreciate you worrying about me, but losing sleep is no big deal. I'm sure once I settle in to the routine, that'll get better. Maybe I'm still in the wrong time zone." The one where bad memories lurked.

"Sure." His dad glanced at him over his shoulder. "And maybe it'll take you a while to see that you could use some help. Believe me, I understand that. When you get the help you need, you'll wish you hadn't waited. I have Elaine to thank for that bit of wisdom."

Instead of tossing his fishing pole into the water to make a loud, satisfying splash, Dean carefully reeled his line in. He'd been mulling over yesterday's revelation that the doctor had saved his father's life. "Care to explain why you couldn't tell me about your health scare, Dad?" He didn't want to start a fight, but he had to know. "Seems like a heart attack or whatever it was would make the weekly update."

His dad sipped his coffee, and Dean wasn't sure he was going to answer.

"Did you believe I wouldn't care?" Dean crossed his arms over his chest, afraid of the answer. Just like that, it was hard to catch his breath again.

"You know, some things are hard to put into words." His father didn't turn to look at him. "Losing my wife was the hardest thing I ever lived through, but watching my son lose his mother…I don't think that's something I'll ever get over."

Amazed at the sting of tears behind his eyelids, Dean tried to clear the lump in his throat.

"I didn't want you to come home," Robert said. "I couldn't stand to watch you do it again. I love you too much for that." His dad sipped his coffee calmly, as though he hadn't just dropped a bombshell.

Watching his dad in the days after his mother's death, seeing him act like the whole world hadn't ended, had hurt. Dean had wanted the loss to show. After that, Dean was eager to do whatever it took to make the new world different from the old one, the one where she'd held everything together.

Maybe his father had been trying to make things better, by pretending nothing had changed. That was something he'd never have understood then.

Dean scrubbed his hands over his face and thought about dropping the conversation right there. Instead, he squatted and draped his arm around his dad's shoulders, startling them both. "Are you insane? You should have told me. I would have been here as fast as I could, and I wouldn't have forgiven myself if something had happened to you. I guess I didn't know how to say that."

His father wrapped his hand around Dean's. "Sure. I feel the same way. Not knowing what you're going through is a real problem. That's true whether you're in Afghanistan or right down the hall. I want you to be happy, no matter what else happens."

Dean choked back his tears. "I get it. I'll tell you more, okay? But I'm going to be safe and sound, rebuilding the Bluebird. I'm glad you'll be traveling, sending me frequent photos so I can live vicariously through you."

His dad laughed. "Right. Send snapshots to the famous photographer. We'll see."

Dean stood up. "You don't have to worry, Dad. I'm okay."

He nodded. "I am, too, thanks to the doc. She could help you."

Annoyed all over again that she'd been allowed to help when he'd been completely out of the loop, Dean tapped one finger on his thigh. "I'll make sure I tell her how much I appreciate everything she did for you." But he wouldn't give up on his plan. He needed this place.

Before he could argue or explain why his case was not the same as his dad's heart problems, he could hear a car coming down the road. "Sounds like the contractor's here."

They both ambled up the hill to meet the guy sliding out of his truck. "Robert, nice to see you. And you must be Dean. I'm Nick." Dean shook his hand and watched his face as he surveyed the porch and ragged front yard. "Where should we start?"

"How about we finish introductions first?" They turned to see Elaine standing on the front porch, hands braced on her hips.

If anyone had doubts about the benefits of running, one look at Elaine in her bright red shorts and spotless white shirt should answer them. He had to admire her commitment to her plans, but at that moment, he was struck again by how well she fit against the backdrop of the Bluebird. He had no doubt that if she were in charge, the inn would shine as bright as her eyes in the warm morning sunshine.

Dean could understand his father's dilemma, too. Given a choice of people to entrust with something as important as the family business, he might go with Elaine. She inspired confidence.

"Dr. Watson, we already know each other." Nick glanced at Robert for direction.

"What the doctor means is that Elaine and Dean here are both thinking about taking over the inn. So instead of the minor repairs I had in mind, we're going to start with a tour, get some idea of the improvements each of them wants to make. And the costs. All right with you?"

Nick tapped his pencil against his clipboard. "They're not renovating together, right? So they're probably going to have different inspiration?"

"Oh, yeah," Dean said.

Elaine smiled at his dry answer. When their eyes met, her amusement was irresistible. He fought the chuckle but couldn't help the way his lips turned up. The thrill of making a pretty girl smile never got old.

Get a grip, man. She's the enemy, not the cool girl you're trying to impress.

Nick sighed. "All right. Let's give it a shot. First priority is…"

"The kitchen," Dean and Elaine said together. She opened the door and waited for them to follow her inside.

"Where exactly are the cabinets?" Nick asked and kicked at the linoleum. "And what happened to the floor?"

"DIY gone wrong. We'll need the floor repaired and the cabinets replaced. Everything else works." Dean turned to move on, but Elaine held up a hand.

"Except if this is going to be a bed-and-breakfast again, the kitchen will have to be updated. New cabinets, counters, stainless steel." She shrugged. "It's what visitors would expect, and I want this to be a gathering spot, somewhere guests feel comfortable hanging out and making conversation. We won't do a meal service, but the continental breakfast will be served right here." Just as it had been when his mother ran the place and the rose tiles in the backsplash had been quaint instead of faded.

Nick glanced from Dean to Elaine. "Big difference in those plans."

"Fishermen will be content with new linoleum and the old cabinets as long as everything works. Besides, those cabinets were originals. People like antiques, right?" Dean said. "I'll spend that money on a new marina, where they'll really appreciate it."

"A marina?" Nick clapped his hands together. "Now that's a project I could get excited about."

Elaine turned toward his father as though she was appealing for backup.

So Dean did the same.

And his father backed right out of the sticky situation.

"Well, now, the cabinets are out in the garage so… Let's finish up in here first. Then we can take a look at the dock." Robert led them down the hall.

"We'll definitely want to take the wallpaper down," Nick said. "Maybe paint a neutral color. White's good. Refinish the floors."

Dean motioned above the railing. "We could mount fish or maybe pictures of big catches. Keep a record that way."

"No way is that wallpaper going anywhere. It's in fine shape, and I like it." Elaine draped an arm over the carved banister, her lips twisted in disapproval. "When I think of the Bluebird, I remember these morning glories. My visitors will appreciate a touch of the past while they're enjoying the new conveniences like stainless steel. That's why I'll invest in the guest rooms." Then she raised an eyebrow.

He could see where she was coming from. When guests thought about the Bluebird, they'd probably remember that wallpaper fondly. It reminded him of his mother.

Watching it go would hurt, but he had to move forward.

The change would be good for him and for the Bluebird.

Again they turned to his father, and again he declined to offer an opinion.

Nick glanced from Elaine to Dean. "Well…" He ran his fingers through his hair. "Maybe we look around outside."

They headed down the hill. "We'll expand these docks, repair the boat slips, add a small marina, maybe fifteen by twenty feet, to sell bait and a few convenience items." Dean walked along the shoreline and pointed at the end of the dock. "What do you think? Wouldn't be too expensive to build here, would it?"

Elaine tapped her foot impatiently but before she could fire off a rebuttal, Robert turned and studied the house. "Block the view of the cove, you mean?"

Dean stared out over the lake. Surely the added revenue would justify a partially blocked view. It would be a big, satisfying change, a way to make his mark.

"Is the marina something you guys agree on?" Nick asked. Dean and Elaine both shook their heads firmly. "Of course not."

Robert sighed. "Maybe it's too soon. New plan. Let them write up a list, maybe do some drawings or something. Then you can quote them separately and save your-self some confusion."

"Perfect. You guys call me in a week or so, and we'll set something up." Nick walked to his truck and didn't look back. He had his phone to his ear as he reversed down the gravel drive, leaving nothing but a cloud of dust.

They walked slowly up to the porch and inside the disputed territory. "We could have at least had the cabinets put in, even if it was only temporarily. Surely we can agree on that," Elaine said.

"I can live with the kitchen as is for a few weeks. Can you?" Dean watched her roll her eyes.

"Of course, but we didn't have to. That's all I'm saying." She straightened her glasses. "Not making easy decisions be-cause we're on opposite sides of the fence is just silly."

She was right. He hated that.

Letting her be the reasonable one was a dangerous precedent. Before he could fig-ure out the best recovery, his father held a hand up. "And on that note, I have an an-nouncement. I'm leaving. Today. Now. You kids can work all this out, so wow me with great ideas when I get back." Then he ran up the stairs, two at a time.

Dean thought about demanding to see his medical records. His dad didn't act like a man with a heart condition.

He acted like a man making a quick getaway.

WHEN DEAN WENT in the opposite direction, right out the door and down to the dock, Elaine considered following Robert and explaining why he had to stay a bit longer. He was her only hope.

If he left...

Well, she would be on her own. With Dean at close range. The idea of arguing with him didn't bother her, but if she got to know him...beating him would be so much harder. Robert was a buffer.

But she'd been fighting her own battles for years. She could handle this.

Elaine paced in the small foyer and lectured herself on getting too worked up over the situation. That was not what the Bluebird was about.

Her phone rang, and she realized she already had plenty of things to worry about. This was supposed to be her new hobby, something she enjoyed.

She stepped out onto the porch, slipped into the rocker that was going to be her chair and answered. "Morning, Mom. How are you?" They made their usual small talk and finally her mother said, "I've been thinking about your inn. Maybe I should visit. It's been a long time. I want to see what you're excited about."

Elaine blinked and then took a look around the porch and yard, neither of which were anything to get excited about. "Wow, I didn't expect that. There's no guarantee that I'll get the place, but you could definitely come for a visit. See what you think. Just give me a couple of weeks."

"Great. I signed up for a cooking camp at the community college. It starts next week. I'll come up after and impress you with all I've learned. How's that? I'm actually taking your advice."

"That is a surprise. I'm a doctor. I'm used to people ignoring my advice."

Elaine checked her phone display to make sure her mother's name was showing. Her clear, reasonable tone of voice was nice this early in recovery. "I'd love to see you, Mom."

"Wonderful. Now, I have to go. I'm going to practice in the kitchen so I don't look like a helpless fool in front of the other ladies in the class. I have plenty of cookbooks to work with, thanks to Jerry. I should put them to good use." Her mother laughed, and at least one of the worries weighing Elaine down eased.

"Studying even before the class starts? What's gotten into you?" she asked.

"Where do you think you got your overachiever tendencies? Your father? He never met a last minute he didn't love." Her mother sighed. "I'm looking forward to seeing you. We've got a plan?"

"It's a date." When she ended the call, Elaine could feel the grin on her face. It was unusual, but she was so excited to hear about her mother trying something new. Something new might be what they both needed.

"A date, huh?" Robert said as he stepped onto the porch carrying a duffel bag. "I didn't expect that."

Stumped on the correct way to answer, Elaine said, "You're packed already? Don't let me drive you away, Robert."

He shook his head. "Nah, got a call yesterday that my travel trailer was ready, so I was planning to leave next week. Get a jump on my journey to the Grand Canyon, that's all."

They were both silent as they stared at Dean sitting by the water.

"Doc, could you do me a favor while I'm gone?"

"Will I earn a few extra points?" Elaine asked with a smile.

Instead of giving her his usual half smile, he scratched his temple. "No, but…you're a doctor first? Before the Bluebird. You'd help anyone you could, right?"

"Sure. Yes. Of course." She felt like the worst jerk for teasing when he had a medical question.

"If you have a chance, see if you can get him to talk. He's… Maybe you can help. You and I both know you're experienced at treating difficult patients." Robert rubbed the back of his neck and sighed. "I would really appreciate it."

Elaine didn't know how she would manage that without compromising her chances of winning, but she nodded. "I'll try." *Sure. I'll just get him to tell me his problems, help him to the best of my ability, destroy my competitive edge and lose. No problem.*

Only Robert Collins could ask this of her.

It had taken the threat of death to get him to make a change. She hoped his son would be different.

Robert waved and headed to the dock. She watched him talk with his son, although they didn't seem to be facing each other. Men were funny, but she got it. Sometimes that little bit of distance was the difference between control and losing it.

They shook hands, and Robert waved as he walked across the yard to his truck. Once the dust cloud settled, she eased back in the rocking chair and tried to let the rhythmic creaking bring the peace she remembered.

Still no luck.

She blamed the new problem her brain had to work on: diagnosing Dean. Old injuries that caused pain? She could help with that. Writing a prescription would be simple, and then she could still beat him without feeling guilty. Probably.

If it was something else, she still might be able to help. If he'd let her.

The more she knew about him, the harder it would be to treat him like the competition.

She'd have to try anyway.

Making a diagnosis without letting him know she was working on the problem would be the challenge. He likely wouldn't thank her for her help, at least not in the beginning.

However, hardheaded men were not a new dilemma.

The creaking of her rocking chair sounded less satisfying, more hollow than it had while she and Dean were rocking in counterpoint the day before, and the porch felt too big all of a sudden.

"I'm heading into town to take a look around." Dean stood at the bottom of the steps. She'd missed his approach completely. When she was working on a problem, the whole world could disappear.

"Okay. See you later."

She watched him walk away, analyzing his gait—which was a little stiff, but not labored—and his ease in sliding behind the wheel. He didn't seem to be in pain, but he might be an excellent faker. His father was.

When the dust cloud settled, she decided to inspect the dock that held such fascination for both Mr. Collinses. It was pretty much Dean's domain. She wouldn't intrude while he was there, but now it was fair game. She eased down and dangled her feet in the cool water with a relieved sigh.

"I believe I get it. The porch is beautiful, but down here it's all so much closer." And she was talking to herself again. She'd definitely have to get a faithful hound when she moved out here, one that would follow her around so she'd always have someone to talk to. "Because that's a bit less crazy."

For a whole ten minutes, she tried communing. She really did. But the list of things to do kept popping up. Each project she finished would make her look that much better. Besides, if her mother came right now, she'd miss the charm of the inn completely even if she could get over the memories.

Elaine stood up and walked to the end of the dock to stare up at the house. "Garage. Let's see what's in the garage."

Finding the key to the garage turned out to be easier than she imagined. It was in the lock. "Nice," she said, sighing.

Whatever had happened to the house, Robert had kept the garage tidy. A riding lawn mower sat in front of double doors, and the missing kitchen cabinets and countertops lined one wall.

She walked over to the mower. "Oh, good. We keep the key in the mower, too." She paced in a wary circle around it. "How hard could it be? Like driving a car."

If it starts, I'll mow the grass. If it doesn't, I'll go back to sitting on the dock. Obviously, it'll take me some practice to get the hang of it.

Getting a jump on the competition... maybe she was more like her mother than she thought.

Elaine opened the doors to find a small ramp leading to the yard behind the inn. "Here goes nothing." She slid into the seat, turned the key and clapped when the mower started.

"Operation: win the Bluebird begins!"

CHAPTER FIVE

TALL PINES HAD changed some since he'd lived here, but a few things could be counted on to remain. One of them was King's Hardware. He peeked in the window and waved at the old man who'd hired him to stock shelves when he was sixteen. His mother had hated the idea of him working a summer job, but all he'd been able to see was money for a car and an escape from the daily chores. Cleaning guest rooms and scrubbing toilets hadn't been his idea of satisfying work.

Mr. King waved back, the complete lack of recognition not all that surprising but disappointing anyway. In his head, Tall Pines was frozen in time. He should be able to step in without a ripple.

Obviously, the town had changed, and some acquaintances had forgotten him.

He paused in front of The Gym to see

an attractive blonde talking on the phone. When she saw him, she straightened and waved. She didn't recognize him, either, but that didn't seem to bother her a bit.

Dean's slow tour of the streets around the courthouse was a nice way to ease back into his hometown. He didn't meet a person who remembered him, so he didn't have to make awkward conversation that would inevitably lead to his accident or some crazy assignment he'd barely managed to escape.

Still, he'd held on to the memory of his hometown like a promise. Feeling like he didn't fit here made it harder to believe Tall Pines would help him find normal again.

Normal? What does that even mean anymore?

A screech of metal and shouting nearby had him hunkering down and searching for the nearest hiding spot. Just like that, Dean had an answer. Normal meant not running for cover at every loud noise.

"Hey, sorry, man." Dean could see a lanky kid struggling under the weight of a ladder. The guy who'd been watching the boy secure the ladder in the bed of the truck offered him a hand. "Sounded horrendous, didn't it? Just metal sliding on metal. That kid is going to destroy my truck's paint." He held both hands up in surrender as though he'd hire better help if he could.

Embarrassed and angry that even in Tall Pines every loud noise made him cringe, Dean gripped the guy's hand. "No problem. Thought shrapnel was headed my way." He tried a hearty laugh, and the guy smiled. Before he could say anything else, Dean jaywalked across the street while he took long, deep breaths.

Maybe he should have tried more than one session with the therapist.

New scenery and new adventures had always solved his problems. This time, he'd needed familiar scenery and safe adventures.

Unfortunately, he'd had a lot more time to think than he was comfortable with.

Normal shouldn't be this hard. And it definitely shouldn't take this long to settle in to the routine of small-town living.

His heart racing as if he'd been running for his life, Dean stopped in front of the newspaper office and thought for two seconds about going in to introduce himself. In a town this size, the newspaper was about the only place he could sell his work unless he tried to license his shots or sell prints. Dean might be eager to give up living out of a backpack, but he'd never give up photography. Whether home was the Bluebird or somewhere else, the world was clearer through a camera lens. Finding a way to make that obsession pay would be a smart idea.

Then he remembered he was dressed as though he owned no mirrors. Another day would be better.

"Hey, I was hoping you'd stop by." A man with a friendly smile stepped out onto the sidewalk. "Mark Taylor. This is my paper. And you're Dean Collins, world-famous photojournalist. It's a pleasure to meet you."

Dean shook Mark's hand and tried to determine how he felt about being called a *world famous* anything. It was only true if the *world* stopped at the doors of King's Hardware. Mr. King had no idea who he was. He was sure there were more people like Mr. King than those who knew his work. But it was nice to know his dad believed in him. "Did my dad visit? Mention I was home?"

Mark nodded. "Yep, on his way out of town. Said I might want to visit the Bluebird. It sounds like you have something exciting going on out there."

"Well, right now it's not much to look at, but in a few weeks, I'll have a solid plan and start making my changes." Dean shoved his hands into his pockets and tried not to shuffle his flip-flops. This guy was no fashion plate, but a polo shirt suddenly seemed like a much better choice.

"Robert mentioned Dr. Watson's out there, too, working on her own plan. I didn't know she had enough spare time for a hobby this size. Seems like everyone in town has been to see her lately. Too bad a cold's not front-page news. Definitely page two." Mark propped one shoulder against the glass window.

Unwilling to talk about the details of his father's crazy plan, Dean glanced down the street. "I did want to introduce myself, but obviously you already know what I do. If you ever need a photographer, you could give me a call." He braced himself for the inevitable questions. People always asked about war and terrorism and the big news items of the day, but no one was prepared to hear the truth.

He'd discovered early on that even if he wanted to talk about the locations he'd been, very few people could listen. Whether it was sadness or anger or fear, the emotions were stronger than anyone expected.

He'd learned to avoid such conversations when he could.

"It's a small operation, so I normally take most of the photos myself." Mark shrugged. "Not that that's what you would call a good idea. Still, I can't pay much. And you might like to take a break. I learned the hard way how long it takes to recover once you've reached your limit."

Dean studied the other man's face. Mark's steady stare convinced him that this was a guy who understood coming to the end of the rope, tying a knot and hanging on. Just the realization that he might find somebody else who understood the pressure and fear, even if he didn't understand gunfire and roadside bombs, made it easier to take a breath.

"Sure, well, I understand. You take your own shots. I can go across the street and work for the other imaginary papers paying obscene amounts of money." Dean raised both eyebrows until Mark laughed.

"Very good point. I'll give you a call next time I have a story. This study of the school lunch program and its effect on low-income families could definitely benefit from a photographer with skill. That would be you, not me." Mark opened the door. "Come inside for a sec. I'll write down your number. You can meet my biggest fan."

Intrigued, Dean followed him in. Two women looked up when he stepped inside. The pretty brunette was wearing a Clinton County sheriff's deputy uniform. She looked familiar. The other woman was sparkling in a fancy dark red tracksuit. Her pale pink hair was the perfect complement.

"This is my…" Mark paused until the deputy poked him in the side. "Girlfriend. This is my girlfriend, Andi. Sorry, the right honorable deputy Andrea Jackson formerly of his presidency's not-so-secret FBI and now a Tall Pines officer of the peace."

The name helped. She'd been a few years behind him in school. Dean held out his hand and waited for Andi to shake it. "It's been a while. Nice to meet the newspaper guy's number one fan."

Before Andi could answer, Mark said, "Nah, she's not the one I was talking about. I'm not sure where she fits on the list. Top ten?" He turned to look at Andi and caught her hand before she could poke him again. "This is Edna. She's my number one fan."

Edna he knew. The color of her hair had changed since the last time he'd seen her, but he recognized her shrewd stare. As he'd expected, Edna gave him a thorough inspection. "Hear you've moved back. You don't remember me, do you?"

"Been a long time, Miss Edna." He tried his charming smile again, and it seemed to work better. Her shoulders dropped. Maybe he just needed more practice.

"Yeah." She sniffed. "Glad you decided to drop in." Dean made sure not to stare at her fluffy pink hair. Edna had been a sharp-tongued acquaintance of his mother's. If he didn't act right, she'd let him have it no matter who was watching. He'd learned that at a Fourth of July picnic where he'd decided to cut in line to get some of his mother's fried chicken.

Mark clapped Dean on the shoulder. "Now, Edna, I'm not sure you're giving this enough thought."

She frowned at him.

"Imagine all the stories he has to tell that nobody in town has ever heard." Mark wagged his eyebrows at her. "You could have a solid supply of news for a long time."

Edna studied him again, her wrinkled brow reflecting concentration. Then she nodded her head once as though she'd made a final decision and smiled. The change was surprising. She went from severe judge to sweetheart in an instant. "Well, now. I do love exciting stories." She clasped her hands under her chin and said, "Tell me one."

He managed to bite back a weary sigh. This was more like it.

Dean ran a hand through his hair and glanced at Andi and Mark to make sure this was actually happening. "Like, now?" He had no idea where to go with this conversation.

Edna laughed as if he'd told the most amazing joke. If he recalled correctly, this might be what flirting sounded like. Weird.

"Come now. Surely you can pull up one story, just to tide me over." She batted her eyelashes. "You've been around the world. What's the craziest meal you ever ate? Bugs? Maybe even monkey brains like that one movie?" She watched his face intently. He glanced at Mark and Andi. They were both barely holding back the laughter.

Just like the smile he'd shared with Elaine, their laughter lightened the tension, something he'd been living with for too many years. He'd been on his own for a long time, the nomadic life of a journalist making it hard to sustain friendships.

Tall Pines would make it so simple. In one afternoon, he'd already found common ground.

"Well, let's see." He had the suspicion that whatever he said to Edna would race through town like a runaway train, so if he said yes to send her on her way, he'd forever be the weirdo who ate monkey brains.

But her grip on his arm said she wasn't leaving without something.

"Once I flew to India to cover their elections. They take a while. I did a little exploring out in the countryside, met a local businessman who thought he'd impress me with his wealth." And his daughter, but that part of the story could be omitted. "We had the finest meal. I think it was seven courses." All of them very American in his honor. And tasty.

That wouldn't end the story with a bang.

"And…" Edna expected something exotic. He didn't have it to give.

"They served baked chicken." Dean glanced over at Andi and Mark to gauge their reactions. Both of them had passed straight faces, headed for full-on coughing fits. "Can you even believe that?"

Edna frowned and studied him closely. "That did not end the way I thought it would."

"Me, either." Dean blinked slowly and then winked at her.

Her lips were twitching when she swatted his arm. "Young man, you'll have to do better than that." She wagged her finger. "And you will." The unspoken "or else" was loud and clear.

"Right now you're late for the lunch bunch over at Purl's Place." Andi stepped between Dean and Edna and wrapped her hand around Edna's arm. "You don't want to miss anything. Now you have something to throw in the pot and stir."

"Don't you manage me, Andi Jackson." Edna looked at her sternly. "Next time, young man. I want your most exciting story, and don't you dare tell anyone else first." She paused in the doorway. "Don't worry. I'll track you down." Before he could decide whether that was a threat or a friendly promise, she was gone.

Dean watched her jaywalk across the street.

"Breaking the law. Flaunting it in my face," Andi muttered. "She's definitely not my number one fan."

"Nope, that's me, beautiful deputy." Mark smacked a quick kiss on her forehead and then danced out of her reach. "Andi's done you a favor. I don't know what you had planned for the rest of the day, but Edna's hard to shake loose."

"Yeah, I had that feeling." He was slightly annoyed until he realized that Edna might be the best judge for him. She wanted stories. He wanted the Bluebird. There was obviously a nice opportunity for back-scratching if he could overcome his emotions and stick with the facts. It would be hard, but making sure he had a solid judge in his corner might be worth it.

"You should understand that anything you tell her will make the rounds lightning fast." Andi shook her head. "And stay out of Purl's Place. Your ears might be burning, but in my experience, it's better not to hear how the story gets retold."

"Good advice," Mark said and kissed her as he guided her out the door. "Don't work too hard."

Andi pointed her finger at him through the glass and then walked down the sidewalk.

"She's going to walk down to the corner, cross the street and then walk back over to Purl's. Setting a positive example for the citizens of Tall Pines." Mark stood and watched her make the whole trip while Dean scanned the office and wondered if he should steal a scrap of paper, write his number on it and toss it on Mark's desk.

"Sorry. You know what it's like." Mark walked behind a cluttered desk and picked up a pen. "Love hijacks my brain sometimes. Don't tell her I said that."

Uncertain where to go with that, Dean took the pen. "Guess I can understand." He didn't, but it sounded right.

When he'd first started overseas assignments, the new locales and people had been a powerful incentive not to settle down. As he'd gotten older, he'd started to understand how thin the line between success and failure or life and death was in his job.

Any woman who loved him could find herself in mourning entirely too young. Even now he could remember the way his father had just shut down after losing his mother. Love was dangerous. It had taken bullets and explosions and nearly getting caught by one or both to make him understand that the danger might be worth it.

His ears had still been ringing and the dust flying when he'd opened his eyes and wished his father was close so he could say…something.

Now he was here. And he understood his father better than he ever had. But he might wish there was someone else, too, someone who could hijack his brain now and then.

On the other hand, loving someone that much meant being vulnerable. He could still see the shadow of that loss on his father's face.

Suddenly too tired to keep going, Dean wrote down his cell number and handed it to Mark. "Thanks for keeping me in mind. This story you're working on with the school lunches, I can help. I've already got some inspiration."

This was what he did. Go where the news was happening and find the shot that captured the thousand words people needed to understand. The realization that he didn't have to go to a war zone to do that made it easier to believe he could settle in Tall Pines. He could be happy here.

"Excellent. The story's important to Andi and the sheriff, so that means I want a pro. And I'll give you a call next week sometime to see if you and Dr. Watson can show me around. I bet there'll be some excitement no matter what happens." Mark pinned the scrap to a bulletin board. "Another attraction in the area's good for all of us. Don't forget about advertising when the Bluebird reopens."

Dean nodded and thought about asking Mark to be his impartial judge. One of the challenges he faced was not being able to predict where people would fall. Mark was a relative newcomer, so he could be more open to change. On the other hand, he seemed pretty popular with the ladies. The doctor might be another friend of his.

That thought didn't sit well with him.

Edna seemed a much more certain bet, even if he had to take a chance on talking about his assignments.

Before Dean could bring up the proposal of a brand-new fishing lodge to test where he would land on the issue, Mark said, "I'll call with work. You call with advertising. Or just to shoot some hoops."

Something else he wasn't used to: making plans. The luxury of knowing he'd be able to catch Mark again to talk about work or music or Edna or whatever was nice. No way was he unloading all his baggage, but maybe a beer and a game of pickup basketball now and then would be ideal.

Whenever Dean was asked if his career was lonely, he mentioned crowded markets, soccer games that sprang up in the middle of the street and the fact that modern communication meant he was never really far away. All of that was true, but it wasn't quite the truth.

Don't start crying on the guy's shoulder. Leave before you embarrass yourself.

Dean cleared his throat and told himself he was not seeing sympathy in Mark's eyes. "We've got a plan." He waved and stepped onto the sidewalk. The tourist crowd had thinned while he'd been inside talking.

The long walk down the town's main street to where he'd parked gave him time to figure out what he should do next.

Sleep would be good, Dean thought as he got into his Jeep and headed out of town.

Back at the Bluebird, his first clue that something had changed was stepping out of the vehicle onto nice, neat grass. Someone had mowed the weeds so instead of a ragged jumble of green patches, Dean was looking at a nice, nearly level lawn.

"We have a lawn mower?" Of course there was a lawn mower. His father had been taking care of the place, just not as well as his mother had demanded. Mowing had been a weekly chore when she was around.

That one simple step brought back some of the shine.

He wished he'd done it days ago.

Not that he'd ever tell Elaine.

Dean rolled his shoulders to ease some of the tension and stopped in the shade of the porch. The dock was empty. The rocking chairs were still. Her car was parked on the other side of the big shade tree, so she had to be here somewhere.

"Hello? Elaine?" he shouted as he stepped inside the house. The bang of the door startled him, and he had to catch his breath before he could hear her faint answer coming from…the kitchen?

THIS WOULD BE horribly embarrassing, but she couldn't just stay here, stuck under the cabinet she couldn't quite lift. Calling out to Dean Collins for help was her only choice.

"Dean? Can you hear me?" The last part was wheezier than she liked, but it was hard to breathe with a cabinet pinning her hips.

"You're full of surprises, aren't you?" His lips twitched as he surveyed her predicament.

Elaine dropped her head back against the wall and stared up at the ceiling. "Could you please help me out?" She'd been so certain she could handle this all on her own. She hated being wrong.

He opened his mouth to say something but thought better of it. In one quick movement, he stood and lifted the cabinet with a grunt. "These things are heavy. How'd you get them in here?"

Elaine took a deep, satisfying breath. "One at a time. The old-fashioned way." She eased up and then flexed her arm. "Wiry muscles."

He offered her a hand. She studied it for a minute, thinking she really ought to refuse, but then decided that saving her from being pinned under a cabinet might be worthy of a truce. When her hand slipped into his, though, she almost yanked it back. His grip was strong. Solid. Warm. He pulled her up. "Are you okay?" For a second all she could do was look at her hand in his. It was nice, a connection she didn't expect.

Then he leaned down to look into her eyes. "Did you hit your head?"

Her crazy, high-pitched laugh was almost as embarrassing as landing in this mess. "Uh, no, just a slow slide down and then the angle… I couldn't get any leverage." She eased her hand from his and ran it through her sloppy ponytail. "I'm glad you were here. I was about to resort to praying for really strong mice."

He propped both hands on his hips. "Dangerous. I would not want to meet a mouse that could lift a cabinet."

"Very good point." Elaine stretched her arms, grateful for the room to move. "But I made some progress." She pointed at one wall. "That one's completely done. Well, except for attaching the countertop. I couldn't get it through the door by myself." She waited for him to congratulate her or make some sort of acknowledgement.

"Wow. Something you can't do." Dean turned to go.

"Hey, wait." Elaine yanked off her glasses and wiped them on her shirt. What good was working so hard if he didn't even notice? "You could help me, and then this project would be finished. It won't take long."

"Mowed the grass. Rebuilt the kitchen. Day one's been successful as far as making your mark, hasn't it?" Dean sighed. "And I've been wandering around, trying to recognize Tall Pines."

Wondering why his comments made her feel shallow for wanting to win the day, Elaine shrugged. "It hasn't changed all that much, has it?"

"Maybe not. Maybe I remembered it wrong." Dean glanced at the three remaining cabinets. "Okay. What else am I going to do with my time?"

More than once, Elaine had seen couples on home-improvement shows enter nuclear meltdown. But after successfully refueling the mower and cutting the lawn, she'd felt invincible. Not even cabinets that weighed as much as small cars could stand in her way.

Elaine had been sure she and Dean would end up in a rolling scrum if they tried to work together.

But she was wrong. Dean grumbled through mounting the remaining cabinets. She bossed a little over the countertops. He grumbled again while hanging the doors, but all in all, it was a successful job. Working with him was easy and a lot more enjoyable than struggling alone. More than once, she had to hide a smile at his complaints, and his good-natured response to her orders made her wonder what it would be like to do something with Dean that was actually fun.

Then she noticed an undeniable tilt to the second set of cabinets.

"Wait. We have to redo these." She reached for the screwdriver and nearly moaned at the painful stretch of muscles in her arm.

"No way. We did a good job. We can't help it if the walls aren't absolutely even. I'm done for the day. I think I'll take a cold bottle of water to the dock and try to catch up on the staring into space I missed this afternoon." He paused in the doorway. "You can come, too. In fact, you should."

"But the project's not finished yet." She could hardly believe he'd walk away like this. It was just wrong. *Do your best. Finish the job.* Her father hadn't given her a lot of sound advice, but he'd scribbled that message in the card attached to her high school graduation present. His wide grin had matched her mother's that day. In fact, they'd gotten along at every award ceremony and graduation, and Elaine had learned that winning was the only way to pull her family together…if only for a brief snapshot.

She'd been sticking with his simple rule for years now. Her best had gotten her pretty far, and she never left a job undone.

"The cabinets are hung. It's a kitchen again. It's fine. Now it's time for a break." He pointed to the door. "I have other plans. I've invited you to come along. Don't make me regret it."

There was no way she could get the countertop off and adjust the cabinets by herself. Not tonight. Her arms had already reached limp noodle status, and if she could stand upright in the morning without a groan, it would be a miracle.

He tapped his watch. "Daylight's burning, Doc. We did good work. Now we goof off. That's the Collins way." Then he disappeared around the corner.

Robert Collins hadn't written that motto in a greeting card. He'd probably modeled it enough for Dean to pick it up.

"Fine. I've done a lot today. No one would blame me for taking a break." She forced herself to let go of the screwdriver. It rolled down the counter and then clattered to a stop. Elaine grabbed a bottle of water from the refrigerator, turned away from the drooping counter, found a couple of ibuprofen in her purse and actually followed him.

She surprised herself with that.

But he'd been such a big help that it was difficult to say no. Besides, she hadn't dealt with Robert's request. While she'd been pinned under the cabinet, she'd tried to analyze what Dean's problem might be. There was almost no way his issue wasn't something like post-traumatic stress disorder. The places he'd photographed would contribute enough stress to make it nearly inevitable.

Understanding what drove him could undermine her will to win, but she couldn't ignore anyone who needed her help.

Elaine was a much better doctor than contractor. Here was a chance to prove it.

CHAPTER SIX

HE WASN'T SURE she'd follow, and he honestly didn't know whether he wanted her company. Something about working with her made it hard to remember that she was a competitor.

Probably the fact that she worked harder than just about anybody he'd ever met.

And complained less than most.

He hadn't expected that.

Seeing her wrung out after a day of hard work helped him understand that she was human. Instead of a beautiful prop for the renovated Bluebird, Elaine was messy with a sharp wit. He'd wanted to laugh at her comments more than once during their short project, but her focus demanded efficient work.

A doctor who decided to mow the grass for the fun of it? He figured she'd have a much higher opinion of what her time was worth. Given the choice of spending a beautiful summer day on the lake or in the grimy, physically demanding world of home improvement, Dean would not have chosen replacing the cabinets.

But it had been more fun than he'd expected.

"Here." He looked up to see her holding two ibuprofen. "Thought you might need this as badly as I do."

"Thanks." He took the pills and washed them down with a swig of water. "Who knew solid wood cabinets could be so heavy?"

"I'm definitely going to have a long conversation with Robert Collins about taking them down by himself," Elaine said as she sat next to him. When her feet hit the water, her relieved sigh made him smile. "Thanks for your help. I was out of steam before the cabinet took me down."

He glanced over at her. Elaine was stretched out beside him, propped up on her hands, her face turned up to catch the setting sun. Her crisp shorts were now wrinkled, and her white T-shirt was covered in the dirt of decades. The ponytail that had started out perky was bedraggled, but she wore a smile on her face.

Being with her shouldn't be this easy. Instead of restless and ticked off, he just felt…tired. Maybe even peaceful.

Her relaxed expression made him wonder if she felt the same kind of peace here. Then he was curious about what kind of worries followed the top doctor in town. Successful, smart, beautiful. Surely Elaine had it made.

He should not have asked her to invade his space, and he should definitely brush off her thanks, just to make it clear her good opinion didn't matter. They were opponents.

But he didn't really want to be alone.

That could be a bad sign.

"No need to thank me, but you're welcome. I would never have guessed you were such a hard worker." When she opened one eye to squint at him, he shook his head. "You're not easy to keep up with."

"'Do your best. Finish the job.' That was my father's advice, and I try to remember it." She eased back to lie against the weathered wood and crossed her arms over her stomach. "We both recognize there's plenty of work to do here, and I'm not sure the cabinets count as a finished job."

"Because we didn't do the work of professionals?"

"Well, they aren't perfect." Her matter-of-fact delivery confirmed his suspicion that she was ambitious in everything she did. Objectively, he could admire her drive, but he was glad he didn't have to live with it.

"I'd rather be realistic. Those cabinets are up. We can use them. There was never much hope of perfection anyway. Do you know how old this house is? The walls are uneven. So are the cabinets. Even professionals would have a hard time." Dean looked at Elaine and decided to follow her lead. He stretched out on his back with his hands behind his head. "Maybe I'll actually sleep tonight."

They both stared up at the clear sky. He took a deep breath and closed his eyes to savor the moment.

"You know, if it's insomnia, I might be able to help," Elaine said quietly. "Even if it's more, you could talk to me. I'm the best doctor in town. I have references." He turned his head to see her watching him.

"You're going about this all wrong." Dean rolled onto his side and propped his head on his hand. "A ruthless winner would be plotting ways to hurt me, not heal me. You should be sabotaging my plans instead of working all day on a place you don't even own yet. Now the best doctor in town is covered in bruises." He ran a finger down her arm and watched her shiver.

He wanted more—a kiss maybe. Or just the chance to wrap his arms around her and watch the sunset. Not alone. Together.

Not that she'd sit still long enough for that to happen.

Elaine sat up. "Believe me, I'm telling myself the same thing. I should keep my distance because I might not win. But this place makes me want to do whatever it takes even if that means getting bruises." She rested a hand on his arm. "And win or lose, I'll help you if I can. It's kind of in the job description. A good night's rest can make the whole world look better, you know?"

"My mother used to say something

like that." Dean closed his eyes again. He wished she'd just lie down and be still. He enjoyed having her near, but he didn't want a diagnosis.

"Did your sleeping problems begin when you came home?"

"No. They've been building. Listen, we don't have to do this. I owe you more thanks than I could ever give for helping my dad, but I can handle my problems." Dean took a deep breath. "I need some time to decompress. This place should be the best medicine."

He opened his eyes to see her nod.

"I can't argue with that. Also, hard work should help." Then she smiled at him. "You're welcome."

Again she shocked him by not insisting that he go for a test or take a pill.

The memory of his father's concerned stare when he'd brushed over his nightmares and her relaxed acceptance of whatever he wanted to say and refused to admit made him wonder if she might be the only person in Tall Pines who could help him.

She listened. She didn't push. And she

wouldn't hurt for him or be hurt by his memories.

Her success with his father suggested she had a knack for handling tough cases.

"We did good on our first day without a referee," he said.

She stretched, and the small bruises on her arm caught his eye. He wished she'd waited for him instead of wrestling those monsters alone.

"Sure. No fistfights or anything. We spent…what, two hours together? That's nothing to brag about."

"Not a bad start. It was good for me to spend some time in Tall Pines, introduce myself to the newspaper editor. I could use the assignments." Work was something he could depend on. Always. No matter how tough the situation got, he could pull out his camera and tell a story. That made him feel strong. Solid. Almost normal.

If this thing with the Bluebird didn't pan out, all he'd have left was the work.

She sighed. "Yeah, Mark's done a nice job since he took over the newspaper."

Dean waited for her to say something, anything else. Mark Taylor probably got along with everyone he met and must have a Tall Pines fan club. Did they have a history? Maybe she was the ex and hadn't quite recovered yet.

If that was the case, he didn't like Mark Taylor as much as he thought.

When she didn't add anything personal, he relaxed against the weathered boards of the dock. Time for conversational fishing. "Andi seems nice, too. I should remember her better from school. It's clear Mark's a man in love."

He studied the pink clouds and pretended he didn't even care about her answer. Then she said, "That's nice. For both of them. They must be healthy because I don't know much about either of them, although Andi's grandmother tells me about all her achievements." She looked over her shoulder. "She used to be sheriff. Worked for the FBI before that. That's impressive, right?"

There was no tone of jealousy, nothing but respect in her voice. Why it mattered whether she'd dated the newspaper editor or secretly hoped to he wasn't sure.

Ready for a new subject, he said, "Edna

seems like she might be someone to keep an eye on."

Elaine glanced at him. "Uh, yeah, understatement there. Edna's my landlord. When I moved here, she rented me this tiny apartment like she was bestowing a most magnificent gift." She shrugged. "And it was, I guess. Cheap. Clean. That's all I really needed."

Dean frowned and sat up. "You don't still live there? The town's top doctor choosing cheap and clean? Where's the status symbol? Aren't you supposed to have a convertible with vanity plates by now?"

She pointed at the Bluebird. "The only status symbols I need are the busiest practice in town and this spot, right here."

"Can you have both? What's going to happen to the practice when you have a hotel to run?" That was more like it. If he could ask the right questions, maybe he could shake her up. The fact that he was really curious about her answer could be completely ignored.

Her cell phone rang before she could reply. She wiggled around and managed to pull it out of her pocket then held up one finger. "Hi, Mom." Dean thought about leaving when she glanced away as if she wasn't quite comfortable with an audience. Then he remembered he needed to look for weak spots. He had a feeling they were there, even if they were hard to see. "A quiche? Way to slowly work your way into this."

The mention of food reminded him it had been a while since his last meal.

"Not a lot. Trying to relax on my day off."

Dean couldn't name many men or women who'd choose renovation as a relaxing hobby, but he had the feeling she meant it. Maybe the doctor should force herself to sit at the end of this dock for a week or so. He wasn't convinced of its healing properties yet, but it had to be better than mowing the grass.

"Great. Yeah, I'm back at it tomorrow."

Tomorrow he'd be doing a whole lot of this right here. Sitting. Breathing. Forgetting if he could.

Unless…maybe there was something to this type of work. He'd see how the night went. Even a couple hours of uninterrupted sleep might be worth sweat equity.

"Love you, too, Mom." Elaine ended the call, heaved a gusty sigh and shoved the phone into her pocket.

"Your concern for my practice is so noble—" Elaine shot him a look "—but I can manage both. I've accomplished bigger challenges than keeping the career I love while I work on a project that excites me. Don't you worry."

"Like what? What would be harder than a demanding job and renovating a wreck?"

She turned to face him. "Ever heard of medical school? I did it on my own and kept my mother on track, too. I built a practice and made it the best in town. I've spent a lot of time learning to do whatever it takes to win."

The look in her eyes held a serious warning. *Be afraid.*

Dean held his hands up in surrender and decided to change the subject. "So, your mom called."

Elaine rested her chin on her knees. "Yeah, we're planning a visit." The setting sun cast a rosy glow, making her seem softer, less likely to spike a victory ball at him. The happiness brought on by her mother's plan to visit lit up her face while her list of accomplishments had just made her seem fierce. He wanted to trace the small smile on her lips.

"We've got plenty of room," he said.

"Good." She stood up with a groan. "I hope my patients can get used to that noise. I'll make it often tomorrow. Thanks again for your help."

She waited for his smile and then walked up the dock to go inside.

Dean sat there until the pond was dark. The sound of the water washing against the shore and wind in the trees was calming.

But now there was something missing.

WHEN THE SUN came up on Monday, Dean decided to try a jog on his own. The day was already heating up when he dropped into a rocking chair and wiped his forehead on his sweaty T-shirt. "And we won't be telling the doctor that maybe jogging isn't so bad after all."

Then he wondered who *we* was since he was all alone. He'd carefully calculated how long he needed to walk along the path around the lake to avoid Elaine. Being unable to sleep was bad enough. Spending too much time thinking about how he'd enjoyed working with her and sitting beside her was a terrible development.

Worse, he was looking at a full day of being alone with nothing but his thoughts to occupy him. "Obviously, I need a project."

He rested his head on the rocker and listened to the creak of the old wood. There was still plenty to choose from. The garden needed attention. Some of his mother's flowers were still there. Or he could go into town and find someone to come out and work on the road.

He propped one foot up on the rail and could almost hear his mother shout "Get your foot off that, Dean Wilson Collins. That's not a footrest."

Instead of the usual grief that had accompanied thoughts of his mother for so long, he smiled as he pictured her shaking her finger at him. Summer had always meant painting, a chore he hadn't really minded because it involved feats of acrobatics along with the tedium of meeting his mother's exacting standards.

"So I'll paint." That meant another trip into Tall Pines for supplies. "Might as well get started." He showered and skipped breakfast to hit the road. Now that he had a plan, he was anxious to move.

Just before he hit the town limits, he could imagine his mother telling him, "Slow down. Tomorrow will come in its own time." She'd tried to convince him not to be so worried about the future. He wished he'd understood the message sooner. He might have slowed down enough to enjoy his days with her more.

The stupid ache in the center of his chest was back.

"And that's the problem with coming home." Halfway around the world, these memories were rarer. Here, something his mother did or said came to mind every time he turned around. That ache made it easier to remember why he'd left home in the beginning.

He parked in front of King's Hardware and tried to tell himself dealing with the memories would get easier.

"Maybe they'll crowd out some of the newer memories." There were plenty of things he wished he could forget, and if Tall Pines didn't work, he was out of options.

"Talking to yourself?" Edna asked from her spot on a shady bench.

Of course she was here.

"Morning, Edna. Hot enough for you?"

One corner of her mouth curled up. "I'm just fine, thanks. Getting started on your projects?" she shot back.

Her eyes were sharp as she waited for his answer, and he wondered what she knew.

"Yes, ma'am. Seems a beautiful day to start painting."

Her eyebrows shot up. "Oh, you paint, too? I just rented out a storefront, going to be an art gallery. Are you any good?" She wagged her finger. "And don't think I've forgotten about the story you owe me."

He stepped up onto the sidewalk. "I'm painting the building, not landscapes."

Edna squinted at him, clearly waiting for a story as his entry fee.

"Since you're here, and you seem to know about the projects going on at the

Bluebird, I was wondering…" Before he committed, he tried to run the reasons through his head again. At her age, she could have a solid relationship with the town doctor. She might not want to get on Elaine's bad side.

Edna stood up smoothly. "Why, yes, of course I'll be your judge. Happy to do it."

Stunned, Dean glanced up and down the street. "How did you hear about that?" Had Elaine already spoken with her somehow?

"I have my ways. You won't regret asking me." She leaned forward. "That Dr. Watson, she's pretty good, but you'll never guess what she told me when I went in with aches in my knees."

Dean bent his head toward her. "Shock me."

"She said—" Edna checked over both shoulders "—if I'd lose weight, I might see some improvement." Her eyes glittered dangerously, and he was sure he'd made the right choice.

"She didn't." He hoped his voice conveyed disgust.

"Well, I lost some weight, but not because she told me to do it." She smoothed her hands over both hips. "This tracksuit was on sale and I had to have it, but they only had a medium."

Dean nodded. "And how are your knees?"

She moved her hand back and forth in a so-so manner. "Now they're good."

Instead of pointing out that Elaine had given her practical advice and Edna had proven her correct, Dean smiled. "Glad to hear it, Edna, and I'm grateful that you can be my judge. I really want a shot at making the Bluebird work."

"Guess you're already drawing up plans and such? Do you have a budget with projected earnings for the early years?" She blinked at him like she was certain his answer was yes.

With an inward sigh, he said, "I could use some help with that." Taking out a loan to reopen the right way was something he'd agonized over. He'd hate every minute of applying for a loan, and his fear of failure would be keeping his nightmares company, but if his plan were chosen, he was going to make this work. He owed his father that. Even more, he knew his mother would have approved.

The cagey spark in Edna's eyes was his first warning. "Don't you worry. I speak bank fluently by now. You came to the right person."

They both turned when Andi Jackson hailed Edna from the end of the block. "Gotta go, Dean. Meet me at the Country Kitchen for lunch on Friday. We'll make a plan." Before he could agree or disagree, she was bustling down the street, thanks to her fully functional knees.

Win or lose, now he was committed. He had a notion Edna would be a stern taskmaster.

Maybe that was exactly what he needed to go up against Elaine Watson, best doctor in town.

CHAPTER SEVEN

"WELL, DR. WATSON, I can't say I blame you. You've been putting in long hours here in addition to your practice. You look... worn out." Dr. Ronald Bell, managing partner of the Clinton County Emergency Care Center, took his glasses off and rubbed his eyelids. "I've got two new doctors over in Lawrence who are prepared to join the rotation, so I can easily cut you to one shift a week." He held out his hand. "Thanks for your commitment."

"I'm happy the timing works out so well. I love the work, but I'm ready for a change." She watched him consider that as she shook his hand. "I'll keep my Thursday evening shift. That should help."

She vowed to not spend any time thinking about being described as *worn out*. She'd been working hard, but she always worked hard. Elaine smoothed a loose curl behind her ear and told herself to take it as a positive sign that she was doing the right thing.

When doctors seemed *worn out*, their patients should wonder about the care they received. She would. "More free time will be nice."

"Well, now that you mention it..." He leaned back in his chair, and Elaine studied his appearance. Crisp white coat. Conservative haircut. Wrinkles at the corners of his eyes that suggested he smiled a lot. He was a successful doctor. Elaine's mother would call him a prospect.

Why hadn't she ever noticed that before?

He tapped one well-manicured finger on the polished surface of his desk. Her desk looked like the leaning tower of paperwork had collapsed on top.

"Let's go to dinner sometime, Elaine. Are you free this weekend? I hope you don't consider a dinner date a conflict of interest."

The precise yank he gave each cuff, coupled with the fussy, slightly condescending tone, reminded her of someone else. She tapped her lips and tried to place it for a long second. Then he cleared his throat and it was obvious that dinner with Dr. Bell would have way too many reminders of her father.

Elaine stared at her folded hands and considered the invitation. Trying to picture him keeping her company on the porch of the renovated Bluebird stretched her imagination too far. On the other hand, she could easily see him at home in the expensive condos on the Lawrence side of the lake.

Rocking chairs were probably forbidden there.

Two doctors. On a date. What were the chances they'd make it through dessert without an emergency of some sort? And what would they talk about? More work? If that's what she wanted, she should stick with shifts at the emergency clinic. At least there she was actually helping people.

"No, Dr. Bell, but thank you for the invitation." She knew she should have softened her answer when he jerked upright in his chair.

Elaine stood to go. Before she could say goodbye, he'd turned his chair away to answer the ringing phone, and Elaine was relieved to have an escape. She went to the small break room to grab her purse out of her locker. It was almost seven, and the sunrise had been beautiful, but after a day in her own practice and an after-hours shift here, she was ready to see a lot less sun. A long nap would be in order.

After she checked in at the clinic. Wendy always scheduled around her extra shifts, but her patients sometimes had emergencies the office staff couldn't handle.

Then she had to stop at the grocery store because Robert's cereal had been fine while it lasted, but real food was better.

The thought of doing all that made her want to curl up on the cot and take a prenap to gather her strength, but she kept going.

After both lightning-quick stops, she made the short drive out to the Bluebird with her groceries in the passenger seat. When the boxes of cereal nearly fell onto the floor mats, Elaine decided the road needed to be fixed as soon as possible…if they ever wanted visitors.

Surely that was something Dean could agree with.

She parked in the shade of the big tree and rested her head against the seat…

And saw a crazy man stretched over the edge of the roof. The steep, old, who-knows-what-shape-it's-in roof of a two-story farmhouse.

"I have two options here. One, go inside, go to bed and hope he comes to his senses before he breaks his neck. Two, freak all the way out. Right now." She was tempted to try the first choice, just to see if it would work. He was a grown man. He made his own decisions. If they were terrible ones that could lead to death by stupidity, then she should accept them and go on.

But she'd be responsible if anything happened.

She grabbed the grocery bag, quietly got out of the car and walked over to stand below him. When a light shower of paint flecks fell around her, she took two steps back, shaded her eyes with one hand and asked calmly, "What do you think you're doing?"

At first, she thought he hadn't heard her. He kept scraping. Old paint floated down. Then he reached as far as his arms would go and eased back. "What's it look like? I'm getting ready to paint."

He'd already made steady progress. This side of the house was scraped. She could see new wood up by the eaves as if he'd made a repair, too. "You were lying about your DIY skills, weren't you?"

He wiped his forehead using his sleeve. "I don't think I ever said I didn't have any. I just don't enjoy it." He shrugged, and Elaine had to bite her lip to keep from screaming "Get down. Get down right now."

"I guess painting's not quite a chore to me," he said, and as easily as if he were skipping down the steps, he swung around and climbed down the ladder. When both feet were firmly on the ground, Elaine took two deep, slow breaths.

"Were you scared, Doc?" Dean studied the roof. "Don't do heights?"

"Why? Were you hoping to impress me?"

Dean scratched his chin and then swiped flaky paint off his shirt. "That depends. Are you impressed?"

His wide grin matched the bright sunshine, and instead of clinging to the edge of exhaustion, Elaine was energized. Eager to spar a little.

She shrugged a shoulder. "Not really, but your dad told me it was your go-to move, daring feats. Ever since you were a kid and you broke your arm, trying to impress a girl."

Dean propped his hands on his hips and studied the blue sky. "I think that was my second broken bone. As I recall, it didn't work very well. Maybe now I have better ways to impress girls, and I hang off roofs because I enjoy it." He wagged his head from side to side. "Unless you were impressed, because then I did it just for you."

When her lips twitched at what appeared to be genuine flirting, Elaine said, "Just... keep your feet on the ground, okay? I don't want to explain to your father why you're in pieces when he returns."

Elaine had helped countless patients through bruises, dislocations and broken bones calmly, rationally. Her pounding heart suggested she might not be as detached with Dean.

Because it had to be anxiety or fear making her heart race, and not irresponsible flirting.

Irritated with herself and with him, she moved around him.

"Hey, wait, there's plenty of painting to do. I'll climb the ladder. You start at the bottom. We'll meet in the middle." He waved a clean paintbrush at her.

Ready to explain she had no intention of doing any such thing and to make a good exit, she looked at him, really looked, and thought she could see something different than his teasing grin. "You got some rest." Some of the grim determination around his eyes and lips had softened.

"Yeah. I did." He ruffled his hair, and they both watched paint chips float to the ground. "I have a long way to go, but it seems like my mom was right. Today already looks better than yesterday did, and the only difference is sleep."

"She was smart, your mom." She gazed out over the sunny lake. "I remember the last summer we came. My parents were miserable, and all I really wanted was for this place to work the same magic it had before. The last day we were here, I was crying out here on the porch when she stepped outside."

Dean tossed the brush down by the paint can and walked closer to stand next to her in the shade. "And she said something that made things better. That's what she did."

Elaine squeezed her tired eyes closed for a second. "She pointed out a bluebird and said that sometimes they fly away, but they can find their way home. I should remember the bluebird, even when times are hard, because they were still here singing."

Dean turned his face up to the sun. "Yeah, that sounds like her."

"I can't imagine how much you miss her. She was special." So was her son. Of course. How could he be any different? Robert and Martha Collins were good people, and they'd raised an impressive son.

And this was the reason Dean was slowly changing from opponent to…something else. She couldn't walk away from him. Watching such a brave man struggle—a man who'd risked his life more than once to tell the world's important stories—made her want to do whatever she could to help.

She wished she could go back to assuming he was a selfish jerk too busy to help his father when he needed it.

Flirting with him, working alongside him…both made it easy to see there was nothing selfish about him.

What a difference a few days made.

Elaine thought about patting his shoulder or hugging him or something, because when he opened his eyes and looked at her again, she could see the hurt there in his expression. "I guess you never get over losing a mother."

"No." He shook his head. "This was not the conversation I planned to have. There was supposed to be teasing, maybe light trash talk. Instead, I'm half a second away from tears over an old wound." And he wasn't happy about it. She could understand that.

She pushed her glasses up. "Well, as a doctor, I feel it's my duty to say that wounds need attention before they'll heal. Otherwise, the scab might come and it might go, but you never get any better."

He propped his hands on his hips as he considered that. "Maybe you should take a dose of your own medicine, Doc. Seems you have a wound or two that could use some attention." Then he smiled his best gotcha smile.

Telling him about her parents' divorce had been a bad decision.

His logic was hard to argue with.

So she didn't. "I'm going to eat this whole box of cereal. Then I'm going to sleep for a week and a half. Then I will come and paint, but only with my feet on the ground."

His laughter warmed her as she climbed the steps to the porch. Inside the doorway, she turned to watch him and saw his involuntary jerk at the slam of the door. She rubbed her forehead and briefly considered putting off her nap to fix the door. Such a simple thing to help settle Dean.

But she was exhausted, and the proper way to fix it escaped her.

She trudged down the hall to the kitchen, ignored the countertop and put the milk in the refrigerator. "I'm coming for you later, breakfast cereal. Be prepared."

Then she made it to her bed, closed her eyes and didn't remember anything else until the sun was low in the sky. After a quick shower and change into the closest thing she had to painting clothes, she devoured two bowls of cereal before she walked around the porch to see Dean on a ladder. "Reporting for duty, sir."

He whistled long and loud. "Sir? I like it."

"Don't get used to it." Elaine stepped back. "You've been on the roof again, haven't you?"

He climbed up another rung on the ladder. "If you didn't see it, did it really happen?"

"I see more new wood up there." And this side of the house was nearly ready to paint, too. He'd been working hard. And he had the sunburn to prove it. "What is it with you Collins men? Never heard of SPF?"

"Real men don't worry about lotions, Doc." He hit a patch of paint and sent it flaking down all over her.

"Smart men who don't want skin cancer do." She bent to pour paint into a tray.

"Less lecture. More paint."

Deciding that was good advice, she got to work, and just like the other day, with the kitchen cabinets, they worked well together. When the sun was setting, she washed out her paintbrush. "You know, there's a way to get some exercise without taking your life in your hands."

"What's the fun in that?" Dean asked as he climbed down the ladder. "The adrenaline rush is the best part, not that there's much of a thrill with painting. I was perfectly safe. I've done this before, you know. My mother insisted on painting the Bluebird almost every other summer, whether it was needed or not. She wanted her home to shine."

He leaned forward. "And she did not want my dad on the roof. He slipped once, and she never let him forget it. Said she didn't want to have to wait on him hand and foot after he broke his fool neck."

Elaine thought it was more likely that Martha Collins couldn't stand to watch the man she loved fall. Something so terrifying would stick with a woman. "I can understand that. He's not an easy patient." Elaine turned off the water and smiled up at him. "She was lucky to have you, then. You're handy with a paintbrush."

His smile slipped. "Maybe. My dad might have felt the same, if I'd actually been here."

"The flipside is that he could have asked for your help. Right? Maybe he was happy you were doing what you loved, adrenaline junkie that you obviously are."

Dean didn't really look as though he agreed, but he nodded. "All right. What would the good doctor recommend instead of hanging off the roof to get my daily exercise?"

"Simple. Let's jog. Tomorrow before I go into the office, run with me."

She enjoyed running because she couldn't do anything but put one foot in front of the other. There were no questions, no emergencies, no phone calls, just the sound of her feet hitting the ground and her own heartbeat. Dean would eliminate all of that peace.

Before her nap and working alongside him again, she'd reminded herself the smart thing to do was keep her distance. He was too attractive in close contact.

But he needed her help.

He hummed doubtfully. "All that effort to go nowhere? Boring."

She rolled her eyes. "I've got a great path. Easy enough for a beginner." Then she raised her eyebrows so he knew she was ready for the trash-talk portion of the afternoon.

"Fine. I'll give your advice a try. Sleeping is good, much better than staring out over the water until the sun comes up. The lake's beautiful when it's dark but not as nice as the inside of my eyelids."

"Weird way to phrase it, but okay. Right after sunrise." Then she stepped inside, making sure to catch the door and shut it carefully before she went to conquer dinner.

"MOM, I HOPE the cooking classes are going well. Anything would be better than three more weeks of cereal." She propped one hip against the crooked counter and ate another bowl of cereal as she considered the fact that her mother hadn't called all day. They had talked yesterday while Elaine drove to the clinic, and she'd been relieved to hear more pep in her mom's voice as she'd described the apple pie she'd just pulled out of the oven.

But nothing today.

While climbing the stairs, she pulled out her phone. Her mother answered breathlessly after the third ring.

"Hey, Mom, I wanted to make sure everything was fine. Did I catch you at a bad time?"

"No, I just got back from an exercise class. Met the nicest person there." Her mother sipped something, and Elaine counted down to the inevitable description of the most handsome man in the world. "Her name's Betty. She's a horrible cook, so I talked her into taking the classes with me next week."

Elaine blinked for two seconds while she adjusted her answer. "Well, that's great. Does she have any idea you're teaching yourself all about cooking before the class even starts?"

Her mother laughed. "I never reveal my secrets. She'll get there and believe I'm some kind of prodigy. It'll be fun."

Elaine wondered if the title *prodigy* could describe someone her mother's age, but she was so happy she let it slide. "Nice plan."

"I knew you'd be worn out. Busy day at work?"

"Not bad. I told Dr. Bell I'd be doing less at the emergency center, and he was fine with that."

Her mother's celebration was loud in her ear. "All right. Free time. Look out, single men of Tall Pines."

Elaine didn't laugh but it was close. "Mom, the single men of Tall Pines? One's seriously in love already and the other..." *I'm living with.* Nah. Her mother would start picking out china patterns, no matter how loudly Elaine explained the situation. "Anyway, there's not a lot of inventory here."

Then she remembered that she'd actually gotten a dinner invitation and turned it down. If she told her mother, the response would be sorrow and dismay. So she didn't.

Besides, it was more of an order than a real request. Those were easy to say no to.

"Well, maybe you need to get out of Tall Pines, then." Her mother was serious as she said it. Elaine had to bite back her first angry answer.

"No, the Tall Pines part of my life is actually working for me. I'll figure out the rest."

After I buy the Bluebird and reopen the tearoom, no single man will show his face here without serious blackmail.

Maybe she hadn't considered her plan enough.

"Go back to the kitchen. I'll talk to you later."

After she hung up, she went to the window to see Dean sitting on the dock again. Even from this distance, though, he looked different. Before he'd seemed so alone, like a man facing off against the elements. Now he fit.

That could be a problem. A week in, and she was connecting with her opponent in a way that made her wonder if she was doing the right thing. She needed the Bluebird, but standing there at the window, she wondered if maybe he didn't need it more.

CHAPTER EIGHT

"SORRY ABOUT THE screen door. Let's fix that next," Elaine said as Dean stepped out onto the porch the next morning. His hand covered a yawn that made her fight a yawn of her own. "Were you still asleep?"

He ran a hand through his hair and then stretched both arms wide. "Yeah. Thank goodness. It's been a while since I managed that."

"So I was right about one thing. Physical activity does help you sleep. I bet you're going to love this." Elaine let go of her right ankle and smoothly switched legs, folding her left leg up to stretch her thigh. He was watching her closely, no doubt impressed with her form.

She'd been running since she was a teenager. She was good at it. "You should stretch. Wouldn't want to get a cramp."

Dean frowned. "I think the only thing

we can count on is me getting a cramp." He put his foot up on the railing and tightened his shoestring. "I've already tried once. I gave up. Too slow. Most of my running has involved wild animals and men with guns. I'm not sure Spring Lake is going to deliver enough adrenaline to make this work for me."

Being reminded that he'd spent years risking everything to tell stories the world needed to hear while she'd been perfecting her runner's form rattled her.

"You're probably right about that. Still could be fun. You've never tried running the way I do it." Elaine skipped down the steps and turned around to trot backward. Showing off a little felt right. "Don't worry. I'll go easy on you." She almost giggled when he blinked slowly. Then she could see the determination chase away some of the fatigue.

When he started down the steps, she set off at a comfortable pace toward the trail she'd found around the lake the first morning she was there. Each step she took made her feel better, lighter, as though the farther she went, the fewer worries she had.

"How are you doing?" His only answer was a wave. Elaine smiled. She was helping him. She stretched out her stride and quickened the pace.

Every now and then she turned to check on him, and he kept pace with her. Of course he did. He wasn't a runner, but one look at him would show a man in fine physical condition. Lugging camera equipment must be a thorough workout.

When the sun rose over the mountain, Elaine checked her watch and said, "We should turn back now. I've still got to shower before work."

"Well, okay, but I thought this was going to be a workout." Dean winked as he ran a circle around her and then took the lead.

Oh, no. This would not do. She'd been taking it easy on him, and he'd been faking all along. He wasn't even breathing hard. All the way she waited for a spot wide enough to pass him. When she came up on the small grassy clearing, she poured on the speed, raced around him and never looked back.

Running at full speed, all she could hear was the thump of each step and the pounding of her heart. This was how she loved to run, all out, with everything it took. She felt alive and strong as she finished the path and raced up the steps with her arms in the air. Dean trailed her by at least ten seconds.

Victory is mine.

She watched him drop down in the shady grass in front of the steps and pant. "Were we racing? You need to warn a guy next…" He wiped his forehead. "Time."

Elaine slowly walked down the steps to stand over him. "Are you okay? You didn't have to keep up with me. I enjoy running fast."

He looked up at her. "I thought we were running *together*. Isn't that how this started?"

He had a point.

"Well…" She had no acceptable answer. To be honest, she was embarrassed that she'd treated their jog like the Boston Marathon. She offered him her hand. "Sorry. You're right. I don't know what got into me."

Dean took her hand and rolled up easily, as though he'd been faking being worn out for her benefit.

"I know. You wanted to beat me. Got a real thing about winning, don't you?" Dean winced. "Maybe we should have jogged together before I got into this bet with you. I definitely need to be on the lookout for sabotage. Right?"

"I don't cheat." But winning a race against someone who didn't even know he'd entered might not be completely honest.

She stared at her running shoes, uneasy with how well he already knew her.

He laughed. "Right. Beating me at a race I didn't know we were running isn't *exactly* cheating."

She took a deep breath. "Fine. I'm sorry. I just…" She rolled the edge of her T-shirt between two fingers. "Winning is important to me."

"And to most normal men and women in the world." Dean took her hand in his, forcing her to stop the nervous habit. "What happens when you lose?"

Elaine looked into his eyes and tried to come up with an answer to that question. She really couldn't, and the truth made her sound like an arrogant diva. "I don't lose."

She tried to tug her hand away so she could put some distance between them, but he wouldn't let go. "Seventh-grade best attendance. High school president of the student council. Scholarships. It's just…that's the way it is. I win. When I do, everything is all right. I'm happy."

Dean looked at their hands. "Are you afraid of what will happen when you lose? Because it's inevitable. You've had a decent run, but everyone loses sometimes. Most of us live with mistakes. That makes it easier to accept them in others, you know."

She tugged on her hand again, and the slide of her skin against his reminded her how dangerous he was. Beating him would be impossible if he became Mr. Understanding, too.

Obviously, he could see she didn't have an answer for his question. He cleared his throat. "Tomorrow, let's do something I'm good at. No competition. Just you, me and death-defying heights. Let's climb." He pointed at the mountain framing Spring Lake cove. "We'll take cameras. We won't look down. How much fun does that sound?"

Almost as fun as her waiting room during cold and flu season. But she appreciated his willingness to ignore her crazy competitive streak. "Maybe. I'll consider it. Probably not. I already have plans to wash my hair." Relieved that he'd put them on solid ground, Elaine decided to postpone the heavy thinking about her drive to win and the sweet idea that someone might be able to accept her, failures and all. Sparring was easier.

He wrinkled his nose. "Aw, I didn't know you were a chicken. How sad for you."

Elaine laughed, and the hard knot of worry and embarrassment eased. "Maybe. That's all I'm committing to."

"Fine. I'll be on a ladder when you come out. Don't look."

Elaine ran upstairs for a quick shower. As she put on clean clothes and left for the clinic, she wore a silly smile, and not even the thought of a long day of possible vomiters chased it away. At noon, she said, "Nina, I feel so good today, I'm going to take a lunch break." Everyone else in the office had a lunch. She usually worked at her desk. Today she was going to get out.

Nina checked the clock. "Sure thing, boss. This is a good time. No more appointments until two this afternoon. Got big plans?" She rested her chin on her hands as if she was hoping for juicy gossip.

"Just spending time with me, myself and I." She considered telling Nina about the Bluebird and needing a judge to vote her way, but remembering this morning's run, she decided to try for a real impartial judge, one who would actually make a choice based on what would benefit Tall Pines the most.

"See you, then." She took off her white jacket, hung it behind her door with the stethoscope and walked out through the empty waiting room, feeling like a girl playing hooky. The sunshine convinced her to walk down Main Street to Jackie's Country Kitchen. She eased around a large crowd gathered in front of the town's new art gallery and peeked inside Purl's Place to see an amazing rainbow of colorful yarns.

"Wonder if Hailey's been here." Her young patient would love the knit shop. So many rainbows to choose from.

A flier that invited everyone to come

in on Saturdays for free knitting lessons caught her eye, so she stopped to consider it for half a second. Then the rumbling of her stomach convinced her to get back on task.

The Country Kitchen was crowded already. She waved at Jackie, a small man with a giant personality, and slid into a booth in front of the window that looked out over the busy sidewalk.

"Hey, Doc, didn't expect to see you here today," Jackie said as he slid a menu in front of her. "Things slowing down?"

"All work and no play, you know?" Elaine smiled up at him and could tell by his blank look that he had no idea what she was talking about. Maybe she needed to start a support group for workaholics in her new free time.

Only if her plans for the Bluebird fell through, of course.

"Okay, I'll have a hamburger, French fries and the coldest Coke you can find." She slid the unopened menu across the table.

"Woo! You must be celebrating or something. The last time you were in you had salad with a side of salad."

Jackie was gone before she could give him a list of the benefits of red meat. The rest of the lunch had less nutritional value, but a lift to the spirits could not be overlooked.

And she loved hamburgers.

So there.

She pulled out her phone and flipped through her emails to make sure there was nothing requiring her immediate attention. Then she realized she was still working even while she wasn't in the office and put it back in her purse to stare out the window.

She had to start sketching out a plan. She'd been spending her precious free time on DIY projects. Those would help her in the long run, but it would take more than mowing the grass to win.

Sitting here in a Tall Pines mainstay made her wonder what sort of plan would be best. Maybe a tearoom and small inn would be less improvement than Dean's fishing camp. Spring Lake was supposed to have some of the finest fishing in the state.

No one said she couldn't do both: renovate the inn and update the docks.

Except she had zero interest in docks,

unless they were for sitting on at the end of a long day.

What else could differentiate her plan? Going back to the way things were might not be as impressive as starting something new.

"Looks like you're hard at work," Jackie said as he slid her plate in front of her next to a beautiful icy Coke. "Lunch is on me."

Before he could race off to the next customer, Elaine said, "Hey, wait, Jackie." Giving away lunch? Everyone knew there was no such thing as a free lunch at the Country Kitchen. Jackie ran a tight ship. Service was fast. The food was good. Anyone who said otherwise could easily find themselves facing a lawsuit.

Her first day in the clinic, Nina had warned her about Jackie, but they'd never had any problems. She'd also never been offered a free burger.

He wiped his hands on the pristine towel hanging at his waist. "Busy, Doc."

"Why's my lunch on the house?" Elaine sipped the Coke with a happy sigh. Empty calories tasted so good.

"For working Mona in last week. She's

been having real trouble with her shoulder, but that shot you gave her worked wonders." He didn't smile, but something around his eyes made her think she was seeing a pleased Jackie. "I hate watching her in pain."

Mona had come in complaining of an ache in her shoulder, the result of an old injury they'd been discussing and watching for a few months. The cortisone shot had given her some relief. "Well, any doctor would have done the same." Elaine squirted a puddle of ketchup on her plate. "Not that I don't appreciate the thanks."

"My Mona deserves the best, and I'll do whatever I can to get it for her." He snapped his fingers at Ralph and motioned at her drink, the one she'd taken three sips out of. "Need a refill over here."

Ralph smiled as he brought her a second glass, and Elaine wondered how many would line the table before she got up. Then she decided she didn't care.

Jackie scanned the diner's tables and then took a step closer. "You aren't going to close the clinic if you buy the Bluebird, are you?" He tapped the table. "That would be an awful thing."

"How did you hear that?" The French fry in her mouth might have made it hard to understand but Jackie probably had a lot of experience translating.

"Edna was in here crowing she was going to be a judge for the 'handsome' photographer." He swiped the clean towel across the spotless table and rolled his eyes.

"Handsome in a rough-around-the-edges kind of way, I guess," she murmured while she considered the possibilities. She still needed a judge. Jackie had never been afraid of making enemies in town, so he might even be willing to go against a hometown boy in order to come down on her side, the doctor who'd helped his beloved wife.

Jackie's support could be the edge she needed.

Before she could figure out a way to test the waters, Jackie bent to whisper, "Heard he might even be planning to open a restaurant. Know anything about that?"

Instead of immediately debunking the rumor, Elaine took a bite of her burger and chewed while she watched Jackie cross his arms and tilt his chin up.

"Probably serve down-home favorites like this burger, things fishermen would order after a long day out on the lake," Jackie muttered. He squinted as if he was trying to peer inside her brain to determine the answer.

Playing fair was hard, especially when she was handed such a golden opportunity. Elaine doubted that the idea of a restaurant had ever crossed Dean's mind. And if Jackie had seen the state of the kitchen, he'd understand that, too.

The way Jackie hovered near her table made it clear he wasn't leaving without some kind of answer.

Elaine shrugged. "Wonder how many people would actually come all the way into town if there's a closer choice."

None of the restaurants in Tall Pines would want more competition.

"Of course, in my plan, the tearoom would serve mostly snacks, maybe some pastries…things to tide people over between trips to town, where they can find real, solid meals." She watched his wheels turning.

"What's he know about running a restaurant anyway?" Jackie picked up his towel and shoved it into the waistband of his apron before he pointed at his trophy case. "Thirteen trophies. All of 'em saying I'm the best chili cook in town. For sure he doesn't have any of those."

"Not yet." Elaine peered at him over the rim of the glass.

When Jackie's jaw tightened, she decided she'd pushed hard enough for one day. Win or lose, she still had to live with herself when the whole thing was decided. "I don't suppose you'd help me, would you? Just imagine, the Bluebird would be the draw it used to be with a tearoom for families and no new restaurant."

"Kids these days… Think they'll be interested in a quiet spot on the lake with no gaming systems or surround sound?" Jackie rocked back on his heels. "Got my doubts, Doc."

He made a good point. Just because she'd loved it didn't mean other kids would, especially now. "What about their moms and dads? Maybe the quiet is what they're looking for. You know, quality family time."

His lips flattened. "Got the feeling you're stringing me along for some reason."

"Maybe you could help me come up with a solid plan, one that will attract families to Tall Pines." She needed a judge. Having someone like Jackie in her corner, a known winner even if he wasn't always popular, could be her secret weapon.

"Ain't gonna be easy, but I figure you and me can come up with a real winner." He held out his hand, and Elaine shook it firmly. "On one condition."

Elaine started to argue, but his stony face convinced her to wait. "I want to be involved at every step. You make sure my name goes in the newspaper article. That newspaper man will be certain to have his nose in this business, and I gotta keep my eye on him all the time."

Elaine thought about explaining that was actually two conditions, but she didn't want to argue with the man who made the juiciest hamburger in town. "No problem, Jackie. I feel good about this."

"You should." He gestured toward the

trophy case again. "Got a proven track record."

The cheery song he whistled as he went behind the counter had everyone in the diner turning to stare. He wasn't known for his happy-go-lucky spirit, but something had put him in an agreeable mood.

"Like this hamburger has definitely improved mine." Elaine glanced around to make sure no one had heard her and then polished off the rest of the burger and every single fry on her plate. Maybe she'd add an extra lap on the trail to cover the calories. Every day this week.

And next week, too. She emptied her glass and pulled out her wallet to leave a generous tip before she slid out of the booth.

Strolling back to the clinic, she passed Purl's Place again. More than once she'd heard Edna mention hanging out there.

Elaine was certain Jackie could be counted on, but what if she could win over Dean's judge before the competition even got started?

Maybe it was time for a brand-new hobby: knitting.

CHAPTER NINE

DEAN LEANED AGAINST the window frame and looked out over Spring Lake. The sunrise had barely started inching up over the mountain, and it had been a long time coming. Apparently, a couple of successful nights didn't mean his problems had disappeared. This dream involved flashes of gunfire and the crazy race across the desert. He'd been crammed into the backseat with three other Americans who were being evacuated when rebels took Mosul. His translator had fled at the news, and the wild voices around him had been impossible to understand.

In dreams everything was chaos except for the pounding fear in his brain, panic that this would be the time he didn't make it out.

Except he had.

The change of nightmare scenery from

the roadside bomb explosion and the ringing in his ears that made it impossible to think was almost a relief.

He was still waiting for his heartbeat to match his carefully regulated breathing.

If there was a universal scene of peace, this view of Spring Lake was it. Nothing moved outside his window. He might have been completely alone in the world except for the feeling the house had when someone else was in it. Elaine had come in late after her office hours, waved at him from the porch and disappeared.

Now at least he wasn't alone. If it all got to be too much, like when he couldn't catch his breath or get his pulse to slow, he could find her.

She would help him.

He wasn't alone.

The thought made the band constricting his chest ease.

They were competitors, but Elaine's steady concern made him think she'd never refuse a request for help.

For the first time since these panics started making every night a misery, he pulled out his phone and thought about calling his father. They were on the same continent at least.

Instead, he squeezed the phone tightly, relieved to have a second option if he had to make a call for help.

"Fresh air. Maybe that will help." Dean yanked a shirt over his head and escaped the walls that were too close with a quick trip down the stairs. He fumbled the lock on the front door but finally managed to get it open. After stumbling over the threshold, he bumped one of the rocking chairs. The rhythmic creak was loud in the silence. Cursing under his breath, he closed his eyes while he waited for the lights to come on inside or for his housemate to yell sleepy insults at him. When nothing stirred inside, he propped his hands on his hips, counted to ten and listened to the croaks and faint rustlings that surrounded the lake at night.

He shoved aside the twist of disappointment that she'd slept through his accidental alarm.

Thanks to the lightening sky, he could see well enough to navigate the yard. He needed to get to the dock. The thought made no sense, but focusing on a goal helped.

Instead of dangling his feet in the water, he paced back and forth, desperate to get control of the fear and anger and disgust that took turns beating him up every night.

Impatience flared up to interrupt now and then because he should have handled this by now.

"Are you considering jumping in?" Elaine asked from the top of the hill. "I wouldn't. Lake monsters might get you."

Speechless, thanks to the stupid wave of relief that swept over him, he watched her carefully maneuver down the hill. When she grabbed his hand and tugged him down to sit next to her in their usual spots, he cleared his throat. "I'm sorry I woke you."

The cool breeze stirred messy curls, and he was so tempted to smooth them away from her face.

"No need to apologize. I've always been a light sleeper, a solid plus for medical residents." Then she turned to face him. "Want to tell me about it?"

Pretending he had no idea what she was talking about would be ridiculous, especially when he'd hoped she would wake up and keep him company. "Nightmares. That's the part of the job they don't warn you about. Sure, you might die." He took a deep breath and studied the dark line of the mountains against the sky. "Or you might have to live with what you saw for the rest of your life."

Instead of trying to cheer him up or say the right thing, Elaine moved over to rest her shoulder against his, a silent sign that he could talk or not, she was fine with either.

And that made it easier to say what he needed to say. "War zones where kids are killed playing in the streets. Refugee camps where innocent people are suffering, and no one knows about it unless we go and tell the story. But there's always a story to tell." When the sting of tears showed up, he got even madder. "I'm not there now. I'm here, safe and sound in this cozy small town with its neat streets. I ran away. Nothing bad can touch me here. Why do I still have those nightmares? How do you stop fighting even though the memories eat you up inside?"

Elaine put her hand on top of the fist he didn't even realize he'd made and squeezed. That was all. She sat there next to him, her touch a connection he needed to calm down and just sit still for long enough to come back to Spring Lake.

"Aren't you glad you insisted on moving in?" His harsh laugh sounded all wrong. "Nursing the resident insomniac through bad dreams."

She didn't answer, just turned to look at him, her face peaceful in the early morning.

"Now would be the time for some excellent advice," Dean muttered, anxious for her to say he was going to be fine. He would be. He had to believe that.

"I don't have any," she said. The regret was clear in her voice. "I don't know what you've gone through, and I can't tell you how to stop the nightmares. It makes sense to me that you have them, so don't beat yourself up over something you can't control." She bumped his shoulder with hers. "If that's part of your issue, just let it go. Anyone who cared about others and saw what you did would have nightmares. That's normal."

"No prescription, then?" Dean closed his eyes and rubbed the ache in his chest. She didn't think he was broken, and there was no "get over yourself" in her voice. More important, she didn't tell him she knew what he was going through. But to her, he was still okay.

"No. Except..." She sighed. "Do you feel guilty for surviving? That's what it sounds like."

"What? Of course not," he snapped. "It's just a job, not a...crusade or something."

"You said *ran away*," she reminded him. "That sounds like you don't think much of the decision to come home."

When he could feel the anger boiling up again, he took a deep breath. Taking it out on the only person on the planet who could sit next to him and listen was a terrible idea.

"I didn't decide. I was sent home. There's a difference." He tried to take comfort in that fact. And he sometimes wondered if that was the only way journalists could leave that job behind.

"Do you know how many people will go to war zones? Not many. When I first started, journalists enjoyed some thin protections, but now…" He shook his head. "You can't count on any mercy in most places." Her shoulder brushed his again. "But I'm good at it, at finding the story. And it's a sickness, checking the headlines, looking for updates on places I've been or feared I'd go next. Do I have the right to step back, to whine about nightmares, when there are still so many stories to be told?"

He expected her to make some comforting noises, explain that of course he had the right to a happy, safe life.

Didn't everyone? And that was where his guilt doubled down.

Instead, she said, "I can't sit on the end of this dock for ten minutes without the urge to be useful, busy kicking in. I feel guilty about taking the day off for a shopping trip. I worry that someone will need me and I won't be available, and then how will I feel if my selfishness injures someone else?" She turned her head. "I don't understand what you went through, and our jobs couldn't be more different, but believe me when I tell you that I understand how responsibility makes it hard to rest."

"What do you do? How do you cope?" This was the key. Getting over the guilt he felt for surviving and giving up meant the difference between fighting the constraints of Tall Pines and being comforted by them. He knew it.

She laughed. "Work around the clock. Kill myself to ensure I don't let anyone down until some days I don't love the job anymore and wish there was something else, like maybe restoring an old inn."

He groaned. "So what do we do, then? Kill ourselves for the job?"

"I wish I knew." She was quiet for so long that the silence of Spring Lake calmed him again. "Maybe…maybe what we do is accept our limitations." She stumbled over the last word as though she couldn't believe she was saying it. "Everyone needs rest, Dean. Why should we be any different?"

Her shoulder bumped his again, and he thought about blurting out how much he appreciated her coming to sit next to him, that she had no idea what the gesture meant. He bit his tongue. Control mattered more when his emotions were so raw.

"You won't believe me when I say it, but you need to talk about what you saw, how it makes you feel. You can't carry this all by yourself. You shouldn't have to." She folded her knees up and wrapped her arms around them, apparently satisfied with her words of wisdom.

"I almost knocked on your door. I knew you'd listen. Then I nearly called my dad."

"What stopped you?"

He had to consider her question. When the answer came, he hated it. "Fear. I was afraid you would think I was weak."

Her snort echoed in the silence of the cove. "Believe me, I don't think you're weak. Brave, yes. Maybe a little foolhardy because anyone who climbs a ladder like you should think harder about the distance to the ground. But never weak."

He didn't know what to say.

"And your father? He'd never think that, either," Elaine added. "But I had to convince him taking care of himself was smart, not weak, so I suspect I know where you got your ideas."

Her dry delivery made him laugh.

"You're pretty smart, Doc." Skating right past how much she'd helped just by showing up would be the easiest thing to do.

But she thought he was brave.

"Thanks for listening, Elaine. Talking to you…" Made him hope things could get better. Made him wish they'd met some other way. Made him want to wrap his arms around her and pull her closer, hold her against his chest until he couldn't remember bad dreams anymore. "It helped."

She sighed. "I know. It's what I do."

Then they both laughed.

"Being alone…it's not easy in the middle of the night." Dean turned to watch her face. "I'm always glad to see the sunrise, but today, I'm glad you joined me, too."

Elaine stared at her hands. "That's one thing I do understand, Dean. Loneliness is hard, no matter what hour of day it is."

Dean wrapped his hand over hers. "Yeah. Having you here has been…nicer than I expected."

Her soft laugh was beautiful there beside the lake, and whatever fear remained from the nightmares faded.

But he didn't let go of her hand. Finding something in common with successful, driven Elaine Watson was nice.

He had no doubt she understood loneliness, and he'd probably never look at her the same way again.

The first rays of sunshine peeking up over the tops of the mountains were a sign that the new day was going to be bright.

"Today's the day we climb a mountain. You said you were definitely going, remember?" Dean said as he stood up.

He smiled as she started shaking her head immediately.

"I have way too much to do today." She glanced at her bare wrist. "I have to be in town in a couple of hours. Besides, there's not enough light. I can't fall off a mountain. People depend on me."

Ignoring the short zing of pain at the reminder that he'd let his father down by being absent so long, Dean said, "We won't climb any mountains." At least, not the actual mountainside. Although, when he opened his camp, rock climbing would definitely be an activity offered.

Dr. Elaine Watson would sooner climb

the ladder to the roof. That much was obvious.

"You can borrow one of my cameras. It'll be fun." He raised an eyebrow and waited. She had no choice but to agree. Otherwise, he'd make clucking noises.

Her gusty sigh said loudly that hiking with him was a huge problem in a way that sitting with him through a long night had not been. "Okay. Fine. Meet me on the porch in twenty."

"Make it ten." He watched her trot up the hill, her muttering triggering a smile, and wondered if he'd just made a terrible mistake. Sitting with her, talking about the things he didn't share with anyone, was dangerous. Sharing a laugh and allowing the heat of competition to sizzle between them made him think he'd never find another woman like her. Elaine's mix of care, concern, pragmatism, ambition and just plain energy for whatever challenges came along was rare.

And spending as much time as he had reflecting on how sweet her kiss might be was the worst sign of all. He trudged up the hill, determined to put distance between them.

When she met him on the porch, he held a camera, his tool for gaining some objectivity on the world. The key to telling the hard stories was the distance of the lens.

She took his beat-up Nikon—the first camera he'd bought himself...the one he'd held on to even when he was able to afford the finest professional cameras—and gazed longingly toward her usual jogging trail. Then she sighed. "What's the goal here?" Once the camera strap was around her neck, she walked slowly down the steps.

After he attached a midrange zoom lens to the top-of-the-line camera he'd carried into some tight spots, he followed her. "You mean, how do we decide who wins?"

"Well..." She stopped, a confused frown on her face, as if she couldn't figure out whether to agree with him or protest that of course she didn't mean that. He waited for her to work it out and decided that in addition to being unfairly alert at this hour, it wasn't right that she should be so pretty in the morning light. He shifted the camera, wondering what she'd do if he snapped a quick picture of her standing there, looking so serious and so sweet.

Idiot. She's a shark with a nice smile. This is a terrible idea. Maybe you don't want the Bluebird as much as you say you do.

He had to get his head on straight. And it was a terrible suggestion, but he'd already started. He couldn't back down now. She'd take that inch and cross the finish line a mile ahead.

"I guess it's possible that we aren't competing this morning," Elaine said and raised an eyebrow at him.

He led them toward an old trail. Even if this was a really bad plan, he might as well enjoy the adventure.

That was kind of his life's philosophy.

The trail wound up to the top of the mountain behind the inn, where he could see the lake and part of Tall Pines.

Or it had a decade ago.

Now everything might be different.

He stopped when Elaine gripped his sleeve. "You aren't going to take me out in the woods and leave me, are you? Because my sense of direction isn't up to hacking my way through forest." She wrinkled her nose. "I might deserve it, but you won't, will you?"

The chink in her armor, her fear at being abandoned, surprised him. And it made him wonder about her own battle with loneliness.

"No, I won't desert you. That's my favorite camera." He waited for her to laugh and then took her hand, alarmed again at how nice it felt. "I won't leave you. I promise."

She opened her mouth but thought better of whatever she was going to say. Instead of arguing or demanding more assurance, she squeezed his hand. "All right. I'm going to trust you to keep that promise." She gestured at the camera. "Want to give me any pointers with this?"

"Sure." He walked around to look over her shoulder and then wished he hadn't. This close, he could smell shampoo and warm skin. "Here's the aperture setting. The smaller the number, the wider open the lens, so if you need lots of light to get a clear shot, lower it. Just remember that the area of focus narrows when you do that so things get blurry in the background."

She nodded, and her ponytail brushed his shoulder. He took a deep breath and rushed through the rest. "Here's the shutter. Fast shutter for action with good light. Slow shutter for stationary objects and low light. If it's a low number, you get lots of light, but the lens stays open longer so you have to be still or your shot will get blurry. That's all there is to it."

Then he marched past her and headed up the barely visible trail. When he opened this to visitors, he'd have to mark it better, or they'd have the forest rangers out here every day looking for hikers like the doctor who thought in left and right instead of east and west.

And the less he thought about her, the better. If she got close enough, as close as they'd been, he might lose the battle and kiss her.

That would be an awesome, terrible mistake.

"Hey, wait," Elaine called. "I want to take a picture."

He turned to see her kneeling on the path, the camera to her eye as she aimed carefully at a wildflower. He thought he heard her mutter, "Low light, low shutter, low aperture."

A beautiful woman who'd listened to what he'd said and taken it to heart in order to take the best shot of a common weed. How was he supposed to hold on to the wary adversarial spirit when she insisted on being so great?

Then she bounced up, as satisfied as could be with her first shot, and smiled brightly at him.

His only defense against kissing her was to raise his own camera and snap a photo of her. That much joy needed to be captured.

"Hey, no photos, please," she said and eased around him. "Don't you know you don't aim a camera at a woman before she puts her face on?"

She hurried up the trail in long strides. Neither the change in altitude nor the exertion of hiking up, up, up seemed to have any effect on her.

"Come on! I know we aren't racing, but I'm winning." He could hear the smile in her voice and figured he was doomed. His only shot was to stall.

"You're only winning if you're going in

the right direction," he yelled and took off up the path to catch her. For the rest of the hike, he was able to focus on the sensation of pushing himself higher and higher while he reconnected with his camera.

He could hear her thudding steps for a bit, then nothing. He had to stop more than once to see the faint blue paint marking the path and eventually walked out into the opening on top of the mountain.

Where there was no Elaine.

"Elaine?" he shouted and turned back down the trail, watching for any signs that she'd made a wrong turn. She'd either been faking her fear of getting left behind or had forgotten it when she'd seized her chance to forge ahead. He fished out his cell phone and saw that the signal was weak. "Elaine? Can you hear me?"

"Just keep yelling. I'm headed in your direction." Even here he could detect the annoyance in her voice.

"Okay, should I tell you how easy it was to beat you when you have no sense of direction?" He propped one shoulder on a pine. "Or I could tell you this cool story I've heard. It's about a tortoise and a hare."

"Ha ha. Funny. And I deserve every bit."

He bent to see her moving slowly through the undergrowth. She didn't look like a winner. If he took this shot, he'd call it "Lost Loser with a Limp." And she'd probably use one of the hundreds of ways a doctor might know to kill him and have the final laugh. Murder wasn't too far from her mind if he had to judge by her glare.

He offered her his arm. "What happened? Trip over your ego?"

She narrowed her eyes at him and then laughed. "Little bit. Twisted my ankle. I can walk it off."

"So much for not competing this morning." He wanted to snap at her to not do stupid things that could lead to getting hurt, but the color on her cheeks convinced him she was already embarrassed enough.

"I forgot." She shrugged awkwardly. "It's like this compulsion I have. Now I can't seem to break it. Thank you for looking for me instead of…"

"I said I wouldn't leave you." He squeezed his eyes shut. "Never mind. Back to the sightseeing."

They walked slowly up to the top of the

mountain where the trees cleared, and he was glad to see the view of the lake remained. "Whoa. This is worth the climb." Elaine braced her hands on her hips and slowly turned in a circle. "Is that the courthouse?"

"Yes." When would he learn that she didn't react the way he expected? He'd anticipated some whining, maybe a hundred questions about the camera or perfect photo composition.

Instead, she'd thrown herself into it and done the best she could.

She would have been a fearless photojournalist, too, but only with the help of a compass.

"But it's quite a bit higher than I really love."

He pointed at the face of the mountain. "We could have come up this way."

She took a step closer to the edge and raised her eyebrow. "Have you lost your mind? What are we? Squirrels?"

He laughed. "Believe it or not, some adventurous types would pay decent money to climb up that way."

She pushed her glasses up. "It takes all

kinds. I'll wait until I meet them in the ER, thank you very much. Besides, I nearly killed myself by bad sense of direction. I don't need any help from gravity."

Amused at her ability to poke fun at herself, he said, "I'll definitely handle marking the trail myself."

Her embarrassed flush was too cute. He pointed at a big rock near the edge, where he'd spent a lot of time as a kid, just waiting for something. "We could sit. I know from experience it's not too uncomfortable." He held out his hand.

"That is extremely close to the edge." She shifted back and forth as though she couldn't decide. He waved his fingers, and finally she sighed loudly and wrapped her hand around his. The closer they got, the harder she gripped, and eventually she had the sleeve of his T-shirt in a stranglehold. When their feet were dangling over the drop, he checked to see that she was still breathing. "You okay? Ankle better?"

She opened her eyes and took a deep breath. "Yes. But I'm never leaving. I'm going to die right here, and it'll be all your fault. I'm coming back to haunt you, too."

He laughed. "Every time I see you like this, I…"

"Afraid, you mean? Is this your version of winning?" She shook her head as if she should have known.

He almost snapped that it was better than running through the woods like an idiot but realized he could be a good sport even if she didn't grasp the concept.

"I was going to say when I see you like this, doing something you don't naturally excel at, I like you better." And it scared him.

She raised an eyebrow. "My failure makes me more likable?"

"Being human makes you more likable." He loosened the tight knot of her hands and threaded his fingers through hers. "Here. I'm afraid you're going to break your own fingers."

She didn't answer, but she didn't pull away, either.

"Being vulnerable is hard." She said it quietly and looked out across the tops of the trees toward the lake that was as pretty from up above as it was sitting on the dock.

"I have no idea what you mean." He laughed when she rolled her eyes.

"I haven't done much research on post-traumatic stress disorder, but it seems a straightforward diagnosis." Now she looked at him, when he wanted her to pretend he wasn't there, but her eyes showed nothing but concern. "Talking to a professional about your nightmares would be a big step, Dean. And if you wanted to take more steps, there's an antianxiety drug that could help, I just know it."

Instead of the anger he expected, he felt tired. "I'll consider it."

For a long time, they were quiet, and all Dean could think of was how crazy it was that this ambitious doctor who never met a challenge she couldn't outrace was sitting beside him and sharing this flawless moment.

She should be annoying, difficult, hard to please and a general drain on his good humor.

Instead, sitting here next to her helped him shake off the bad night and focus on the future.

"Jackie told me that Edna's going to be

your judge." And just like that she helped him regain his footing, too. "I asked him to be mine." She smiled at him. "Also, you're planning to open a restaurant that will draw all the boaters on the lake, keeping them from making it into town to eat at the Country Kitchen."

Dean would swear he could see a twinkle in her eye.

"Why would I do that? A restaurant would be a headache and a half." Then he realized he had no real hope of winning her judge and laughed. "Never mind. I got it." He traced his thumb across her delicate wrist as he considered the possibility. "At least I have Edna on my side. I'm paying her in a way you can't match—juicy stories."

"If only I weren't so ethical," Elaine said and kicked her running shoe against the rock. "I have all kinds of delicious, expensive stories that Edna would love."

"Too bad." Dean rested their hands on his thigh and wondered if she even realized he was still holding her hand. "Since you called her fat, I'm sure juicy stories are the only thing that could save you now."

Elaine's head whipped around, her eyes

huge as she said, "I said what? No way. I wouldn't." She pointed to herself. "Good doctor here." Then she narrowed her eyes. "She told you about her problem with her knees, I guess."

"Yeah."

"And did she say that she felt better when she followed my advice?" Elaine inched forward to look into his eyes until she realized how close the rock was to the edge of the cliff.

"No. She mentioned that she lost weight to fit her new tracksuit, and then she felt better." He shrugged. "I think Edna believes more in the restorative power of high fashion."

Her lips twitched as she sighed. "Right. Couldn't be common sense."

Dean looked out across the lake.

"Edna's going to be a tough sell, but that's okay. I have other tricks up my sleeve." Elaine tightened her hold on his hand. "Now, get me off this rock. I have a bed-and-breakfast to win, and the day's wasting."

He didn't want to move. He didn't want to leave this pocket of the world where it was only the two of them, but she started to inch closer to the edge.

After he hustled to help her, he followed her down the trail. Like he'd done so often before, he assessed his surroundings, looking for interesting shots and lighting and all the things that a photographer could see that the rest of the world might miss. More than once he was impressed as he watched her stop and study objects and scenes to determine the proper vantage point to shoot from.

"Of course you're good at this. Why did I have any doubt?" he said.

"What are you talking about?" she asked as she concentrated on a shot of a tree trunk. "You haven't seen any of the pictures yet. What if I have my finger on the lens in every one?"

She flawlessly negotiated the turns on the hard-to-see path, stopped for two more shots and beat him to the bottom.

He let her beat him to the bottom, of course.

They both climbed the steps to the front porch, and she reluctantly held out the camera.

"I don't know if I got anything interesting, but it was fun to play." She stepped back when he took the camera. "That's a competition I'd lose—best photograph." Her shy glance away confused him.

And the urge to kiss her had returned.

"I guess I better get dressed to go into town." She put her hand on the screen door and briefly looked up to meet his stare.

"One question before you go." He pointed at the barely there path. "Uh, you didn't have much trouble getting down the mountain even though the path was sketchy. Why were you so afraid I'd leave you? And why would you race ahead?"

"Oh, you know me, trying to make sure I wouldn't lose," she said, pulling the door open too quickly. And she stepped inside, carefully closing the screen door behind her.

Dissatisfied with her answer, he said, "Afraid of the truth? I thought that was my problem. Unbelievable."

She mumbled something he was glad he couldn't decipher and snapped, "Fine. I've been on the trail before, with my dad. I kept slowing him down, hunting for the perfect leaf for my collection." She tilted her chin down. "Don't judge. I had an impressive dried leaf collection for a nine-year-old. He got tired of waiting for me, said he'd meet me at the bottom." She glanced at the creases she was folding in the hem of her shirt. "I had a lot more trouble finding my way that time. But I did it. By myself."

"But you shouldn't have had to. Isn't that what you told me this morning?"

Their eyes met through the screen, and he thought he could see tears, but her smile was bright. "Well, it was a valuable lesson. If I can't keep up, I'll get left behind. So now, I'm the one in front."

Dean thought about that and wondered if it was hard to make friends when everyone was competition.

"You know, there are some things that matter other than winning. Friendship is nice." He studied her closely.

"Learning how to follow would also come in handy now and then." She fidgeted with her shirt again. "Like when I don't know where I'm going and the trail's not marked."

He smiled and then waited until she'd

disappeared up the stairs to have a seat in the rocking chair.

Picturing her as a young girl in glasses with a collection of dried leaves was easier than he would have expected. He'd never given it much thought, but it made sense that she'd be as unusual a girl as she was a woman.

A place like this, with plenty of room to explore and all kinds of scientific wonders to discover, must have seemed like a paradise. Not to mention the unlimited array of leaves to be dried.

While he'd been looking for the highest point to jump off—and almost anyone to watch him with bated breath, usually his mother—Elaine had been studying the world.

And learning to be afraid of getting left behind.

He took a deep breath and wondered if maybe they'd both been struggling to deal with that fear. She'd learned to take care of herself and lead the way.

He'd learned to be a moving target.

He finally understood Elaine's love of

the Bluebird. This place would endure. It was something solid she could count on.

If he didn't need it so badly, he might be glad she'd found her way back.

CHAPTER TEN

"THIS IS PROBABLY a bad idea." Elaine pushed her glasses up on her nose and slid out of the car. Somehow she'd managed to snag a parking spot around the corner from Purl's Place, an impressive feat on a busy Saturday morning. She'd taken that as a positive sign.

Until she'd imagined walking into the store to greet a large group of women.

She wasn't afraid…

She was just better one-on-one.

After that hike and the connection she'd felt to Dean, Elaine had to get out of the house. Retreat was the only way she'd track down her will to win.

Now it was time to get her head in the game. She needed to forget Dean's sympathetic expression—the one that made her feel so vulnerable—and her growing certainty that he meant what he said. He needed the Bluebird.

But for how long? And if he lost, would he return to the work he was so good at? The same job that had left him with nightmares?

His love of the place had been easy to see there on the top of the mountain, away from what had to be painful memories that stirred the ashes of his grief.

She'd only been a visitor and still she sometimes expected to see Martha Collins at work in her garden. Under the ragged exterior, her spirit lingered here. Did Dean feel the same way? Did being at the Bluebird bring back painful memories of his mother?

Elaine looked in the window of the cutest children's clothing boutique until she saw the saleswoman, one of her patients, wave. Then she pretended it was a totally normal thing to be staring blankly at a stuffed turtle.

She'd dreamed, hoped and been disappointed more than once by both her parents. Learning that people didn't change, not even if she wished they would, had been a hard lesson, but she appreciated it anyway. Dean had left Tall Pines because it hurt too much to stay, and he needed the excitement of a dangerous career. Could he really be content here now?

One big difference between her and Dean was his roots.

He was a part of the Bluebird's history. No matter how much he wanted to see the world, the Bluebird would call him home eventually.

And that worried her.

Because now that he'd found the right reason to stay, she'd have a hard time making him go.

Maybe she didn't really want him to go.

Getting to know him better made it even harder to imagine the Bluebird without him.

She'd forgotten about the hiking trails behind the inn, and she'd never made it to the top of the hill to see the lake or Tall Pines. Without him, she might never have explored that far or tried her hand at photography.

Without him, she would have been content to run the same trail every day.

"And I wouldn't be here trying to procrastinate my way out of this by thinking too hard." She checked over her shoulder to make sure no one saw her talking to herself, shook out the loose skirt of her sundress and took a deep breath. Then she pushed her shoulders back as if she hadn't a single fear in the world, a pose she'd learned very young and used to its full effect often, and marched around the corner and straight into Purl's Place.

Whatever conversation was flowing before the door opened came to a sudden stop. Six women turned to look at her, and Elaine had to fight the urge to step right back outside.

"Dr. Watson, come in." Sue Jackson beckoned her closer with a wave. She rolled away from the table and moved her wheelchair closer to Wanda Blankenship. "We've got plenty of room for one more."

The chill coming from Wanda was evident.

"Exactly what is your problem?" Andi asked. She sat at the corner of the table, next to a box of pastries. Wanda glanced in her direction and then thrust a coffee cup at her. "I need a refill."

Andi narrowed her eyes but filled Wanda's cup. "Haven't you heard caffeine's bad for you?"

Wanda, owner of the town's gym, flexed her arm. "Doesn't seem to be hurting me any."

"Might actually win the half marathon if you cut back, though," Edna muttered and glanced across the table at Elaine, the corners of her mouth turned up. Before Wanda could answer, Andi shoved the box of cinnamon rolls in her direction. "Here. We all know why you came, and it's certainly not the knitting."

"Or the company," Wanda answered before she took a bite of the cinnamon roll.

Tammy, the owner of Purl's Place, held out a chair. "Come sit next to me, Dr. Watson. Then we'll see what we can help you with."

"Ah, great. Please call me Elaine." She eased into the chair and set her purse carefully in her lap. "And I was hoping someone could give me a knitting lesson."

Tammy clapped. "Woo hoo! Nothing I love better."

Everyone at the table watched her jump up and bustle around, a blonde whirlwind and the only thing stirring in the shop.

"Here. Eat one of these. Save me from myself." Andi slid a plate with a cinnamon roll across the table along with a cup of coffee. "Better seize your chance. She'll have you knitting and purling presently and steal every bit of cash in your wallet before you leave."

"Seems a sheriff's deputy ought to put a stop to that." Sue didn't look up from the yarn in her lap.

"Oh, Gram, I'm the easiest target at this table." Andi picked up the yarn in front of her, and Elaine was slightly alarmed at the number of needles poking out. "I have a sock yarn problem. There is no support group for me." Andi winked at her and rolled her eyes at Edna's sniff.

"I might have made a horrible mistake," Elaine said. "That many needles would only stress me out, and I was looking for a relaxing hobby."

Miss Margaret, Edna's best friend and

usual partner in crime, laughed. "Well, I'm not sure Andi's the one to talk to about relaxing hobbies. She takes her knitting seriously."

"And I have the kink in my neck to show for it," Andi muttered as she massaged her shoulder.

"We don't all have to knit like Andi, so not to worry," Tammy said as she slid in next to Elaine. "Plus, you only need two needles."

Elaine surveyed the women seated at the table. "Maybe I should try whatever Sue is doing first."

Tammy gave her a shoulder bump. "Now, don't give up before you've even given it a shot, Doc…Elaine." She pulled a loose end out of the skein of yarn. "You're a doctor. You can handle some knitting. Don't worry. Then you can tell all your patients with high blood pressure to give Purl's Place a visit."

Elaine wondered if maybe she shouldn't expand her Bluebird team. Jackie had sound advice, but Tammy seemed to be a real entrepreneur. Also, she was good at mustering the troops. Tammy picked up Elaine's hand.

"First things first, let's make a slip-knot." Tammy pooled the yarn in a circle in her hand, slipped a knitting needle in and pulled up a knot as though it was the easiest thing in the world. "Here. You try."

Feeling the weight of every stare, Elaine concentrated on the yarn in her hand and tried to replicate the knot, very aware of the wrinkle on her forehead.

Everyone's watching you. It's so easy. Everyone here knows it's easy and can do it in a snap. Concentrate. Get this right.

She tried for the same motion Tammy used. "Hmm, no knot."

Tammy took everything from her and demonstrated again. Over and over they traded the knitting needle and yarn, and eventually the conversation resumed. Obviously, the novelty of watching someone learn to knit faded when said someone couldn't get past the first knot.

Already on the verge of giving up, Elaine was grateful for the return of the conversation.

Until it turned to Dean.

"Anybody had a chance to talk to Dean Collins?" Andi asked. "Given him the Tall Pines welcome?"

"I saw him on the street but he didn't come in the gym," Wanda answered with a mouth full of cinnamon roll. "Seemed like he needed a new wardrobe more than a gym membership anyway."

Elaine paused to consider that. "He's perfectly fit. We've jogged together." She smiled at Wanda. "He finished second, but he doesn't have as much practice." She really couldn't defend his wardrobe, though. It was pretty awful.

Still, she hadn't given it much thought since the day they'd met.

When she glanced up to see everyone at the table watching her, their raised eyebrows indicating entirely too much interest, Elaine realized she was defending her opponent.

She'd come to win over his judge, not give the biggest gossip in town the idea that she had a thing for Dean Collins. Distracted, she poked Tammy with her next knot attempt.

"Okay, why don't we come back to that?"

Tammy made a knot. "Let's learn to cast on." She threaded the yarn through her fingers. "Here's how you do it."

Elaine could tell that Tammy had slowed down, but keeping up with the needle wasn't as simple as she'd hoped.

"Boy's got a good plan for the Bluebird, or he will when he works in my suggestions." Edna didn't look up from her knitting, but Elaine had a sense that whatever the woman said was aimed directly at her. "And I like it when people come home."

Andi mumbled something in response to that.

"Well, no matter what happens, I'll be happy to have it open again," Sue said. "Such a gorgeous spot. We used to have holiday picnics out there when I was a child. I still remember that cove."

"When I get the tearoom open again, you should visit," Elaine said, her mind filled with visions of hosting Sue Jackson, Andi, Tammy and maybe the rest of the Purl's Place ladies. Even Wanda would be tolerable from her own front porch.

She glanced up to see Sue smiling at her. "I'd enjoy that."

The opportunity to actually host friends and family was something she'd never thought much about, probably because she'd always considered herself too busy for dinner parties or girls' nights out. With a home like the Bluebird, showing it off would be a pleasure.

When she'd hopelessly knotted the yarn and could no longer pull the needle through, Tammy took it from Elaine. "Maybe let's try a knit stitch. That's super easy."

In half the time it had taken Elaine to create a nest of knots, Tammy made a neat line of stitches on the needle and then showed her how to insert the needle, wrap the yarn and pull up another stitch.

"Well, I've spent some time with Dean, and I like him." Edna raised her chin. "Even if his stories need some spice. I'm hoping I can get him to loosen up. He seems tense." She and Edna traded a long look. Edna wanted to know more about what made Dean tick, but that was one thing Elaine wouldn't do, even to win another judge.

Get back on track, Elaine. Don't forget what you're here for.

"Edna, what is that you're making? I love the color."

"A hat. That's all I knit." Edna held her knitting up and smoothed out the stitches. "Short. Simple. Quick. That's how I like my projects."

"How do you manage to wear them all?" Elaine asked, wondering if she needed to learn to knit hats next.

Edna studied her carefully as if she had to be sure Elaine wasn't making fun of her. Then she sat very tall, her shoulders back. "I donate them to a children's hospital. Most knitters make tiny preemie hats but I knit things for the big kids. They need some cheering up, too." She glowered at each woman. Everyone nodded as if they wouldn't dare argue.

"That's awesome. Someday, if I learn how to make more than a mess, I'll try a hat or two."

She couldn't help but admire Edna's work. Then she watched her last stitch fall off the tip of her knitting needle. Already regretting the decision to try this, Elaine refocused and successfully knit across the row. Her flush of satisfaction eased some of the tension, and she whispered, "I did it."

Tammy clapped. "Hey, nice job! I knew you'd be a natural. Here's how you do the next row." She took the needles, turned the knitting and handed them to Elaine. "Now, do the same thing all the way across. Then you'll have a garter stitch row."

Andi frowned. "Edna, maybe you could finish the story you were telling before Elaine walked in, the one after the boring baked chicken one. We were climbing a mountain somewhere near the Dalai Lama." She smiled brightly at Elaine. "Edna's stories have recently taken on an international flair. We like her new friend."

Edna turned to look at Andi. "You are lucky I take my loyalties seriously, Andi Jackson. I haven't forgotten our truce, but you do strain my patience."

"Aw, the feeling is mutual," Andi said and wrapped an arm around Edna's shoulders.

Tammy snorted a laugh, and everyone around the table smiled.

Even Edna.

"My new friend is a wonderful photographer, gonna make the gallery a success right along with his fish camp." Edna nodded her head once sharply. "I'll see to that."

Elaine wondered what Edna had in mind. Maybe some landscapes, things to sell to the tourists? That was a great scheme.

"Should have known owning every rental property in town wouldn't be enough to keep you satisfied after you retired," Miss Margaret said mildly, her needles flashing in the sunlight.

Elaine was impressed with her speed. She managed to jam a needle under a yarn loop and sawed it through to shove the loop off the end.

"Did you give her bamboo needles, Tammy? She's bound to start a fire, rubbing 'em together like that." Sue winked at Elaine.

"Maybe try to wrap the yarn looser, Dr...Elaine." Tammy scooted closer and demonstrated a loose loop. "You're doing great."

"Got a plan together for the Bluebird, Dr. Watson?" Edna asked. "Seems like you might be working on that instead of—" she motioned vaguely at the growing horror in Elaine's hands "—making a mess. Dean's been sprucing the place up while he's waiting on this silly contest to be settled."

"You know, Edna, I have a hard time believing how quickly you've taken up with Dean," Sue murmured. "Only other person I remember you adopting this way is the newspaper man. You aren't…love struck, are you?"

Edna straightened in her chair and dropped her knitting in her lap. "Sue Jackson, you've gone entirely too far. If I hear that rumor making it around town, I will know exactly who started it."

"What a change of pace," Andi murmured. "Pot, kettle, I'm not sure. I'm so confused."

Edna tapped a finger on the table and said, "He asked for my help, that's all. And he was born and raised in Tall Pines." She crossed her arms over her tracksuit as though that settled it.

"But a fish camp?" Miss Margaret grimaced. "Not sure that'll really attract the best customers for the rest of the town, you know? Families would be better for the restaurants and the shops on Main. Plus, you won't find one single fisherman visiting your art gallery unless you're going to mount their catches for all the world to see."

Elaine could have hugged Miss Margaret. She'd come to Purl's Place hoping to build a relationship with Edna, although after years of exchanging the barest of communication about repairs and rent and the infamous conversation about losing weight, she was sure it would take a miracle.

She considered the four rows of garter stitches she'd managed and poked her finger through a truly gnarly hole. No miracle here.

But Miss Margaret had given her something to consider. Elaine needed to get serious about her plan and how it could affect the town. Jogging and hiking with Dean might be more fun than she'd expected, but it was also a distraction

Had that been his plan? Take her focus off the prize to better his chance of winning?

Of course not. She was more likely to

plot like that than Dean. He didn't need sneaky tricks anyway. He was the heavy favorite.

Before she could capitalize on Miss Margaret's opening, sunlight flashed on silver scissors as Tammy cut the yarn Elaine was holding. "Start over. Practice is good for you."

Elaine was dumbfounded for a long second as she stared at the limp end of the yarn she'd been about to wrap around her needle. Then she looked across the table to see Andi doing her best not to laugh. "She's ruthless, Elaine. She'll have you purling like a champ before you leave today. Just go with it."

Elaine glanced at an innocent Tammy, who was clearing away the empty plates. Then she set her jaw and managed to create her own slipknot on the third attempt. No matter how she held her tongue, she couldn't get the cast on right, so Tammy whipped out the stitches and handed her the needle. "Now knit."

Blinking, but afraid to disobey orders, Elaine tried to keep all the instructions in mind and managed to knit.

Then she got the conversation back on track. "Funny you should mention the families, Miss Margaret. I really want to focus on attracting families. That's the key to winning." She met Edna's stare. "That's why I fell in love with the Bluebird years ago. That's what led me back to Tall Pines."

The tension in the small room turned up a notch as Edna pursed her lips. When she didn't argue, Elaine wasn't sure whether Edna couldn't refute her point or was building a head of steam.

"Martha was so skillful at making sure everyone felt welcome," Sue said and shook her head sadly. "Hated to see the inn shut down, but Robert…he didn't have the same touch." She looked across the table at Elaine. "Does his son?"

Here was a lovely opportunity to do some careful spin on Dean, paint him as a restless kid only dabbling in the project until the next shiny thing distracted him. Maybe she could convince the judges to take a chance on her instead, the solid doctor, a stable, respected member of the community for years.

Or she could go with the truth.

"Well…" She carefully set the needles and yarn down on the table in front of her. "I would say he has as much of the spark as I do. We both love the place even if we want different things for it."

"He's going to capitalize on the location and the fishing, something we know brings people to Tall Pines. What are you going to do?" Edna raised her eyebrows. Elaine wasn't sure whether it was a dare or an attempt to get extra information.

"I want to restore it. I loved the Bluebird, and I only want that feeling back." She shrugged. "We'll rent the rooms, run the tearoom from the front porch and generally welcome tourists to Tall Pines. Why change something that worked so well?"

Sue rested her hand on Elaine's. "Honey, things change. Nothing you can do about it. Whatever you do will never make that place the same as it was." Her sympathetic eyes made Elaine want a hug desperately. "Change happens, but it's nothing to be afraid of. You have to learn that."

Elaine didn't know how to respond. She was afraid Sue Jackson had hit upon the fatal flaw in her plan, so she picked up her knitting. "Okay, I'll take suggestions then." Fighting tears, she smiled around the table without making eye contact. "What could I do to attract families? That's what I want, somewhere for families to get stronger, not a place for men to escape their wives and children." Then she managed to meet Edna's stare head-on and felt a jolt of surprise at the understanding she could see there.

"Free Wi-Fi." Miss Margaret pointed a finger around the table. "That's all I know about kids these days. You have to have it. If you don't, you better not expect visits from anyone older than three without a whole lot of complaining."

Everyone laughed and Elaine said, "Making a mental note, Miss Margaret. I'll make sure my internet connection is solid." She held up her needles. "And I'm certainly going to add knitting lessons to my menu of activities."

"For you or the guests?" Tammy asked as she held up Elaine's ragged swatch and peeked at her through the hole. "Because I don't think you're up to giving lessons yet."

"Good point." Elaine reached into her

purse and pulled out her wallet. "Here. Take this. I need to empty my wallet."

Tammy clapped her hands. "Let me help. I love to empty wallets." After less than five minutes, Tammy had pulled down four skeins of yarn, two more sets of needles, three impressive books with lots of how-to instructions, a video for beginners and a tape measure shaped like a sheep for "fun." Then she rang all the items up, swiped Elaine's credit card and handed her a nice, neat bundle. "We're here every Saturday, just like this. You can also come by during the week for help. Or more yarn." She winked. "Welcome to the sisterhood."

Andi laughed. "We'd start a Yarnaholics Anonymous meeting, but no one wants to quit."

Elaine listened to them giggle and realized this might be the first time she'd ever been part of a fun, friendly group. Some of them were patients. Two or three of them were old enough to be her grandmother. Since she'd lost both sets of grandparents as a little girl, she enjoyed spending time with Sue and Miss Margaret. Edna had never given her the grandmotherly vibe.

Andi and Tammy were her age, but they didn't really have much in common.

On paper, building a friendship with them seemed like a long shot.

But in real life, they'd already bonded.

Over a love of yarn.

And she'd destroyed that yarn, but they didn't seem to think any less of her.

She would never have guessed that would be the outcome when she'd been making her plans to divide and conquer Dean's team. Edna was still solidly in his corner, but even she had thawed.

"Next visit, you'll have to master the purl stitch," Edna said. "Then you can knit anything you want." She didn't really smile as she said it, but the temperature in the room had risen a bit.

"Might need to put up a few shelves in the apartment if my collection keeps up this pace," Elaine said. Then she realized that would only be necessary if she lost the bet.

And she wasn't planning to lose.

Thinking like that would end her chances before they even made it to the final judging.

"Or maybe I'll turn one of the guest rooms into a yarn closet." She smiled at Tammy. "Thank you for the lesson."

"Thank you for your credit card. You two should visit often." Tammy winked and then glanced at Andi. "You might have some help keeping Purl's Place in business."

"Thank goodness," Andi murmured fervently.

"More money for the wedding, right, Andi?" Every head in the room turned in Andi's direction, stirring up a surprisingly strong breeze. Elaine paused with her hand on the door to see what happened next.

"Gram, there is no wedding. Mark and I, we have to take things slowly. And…" Andi scrutinized the table "…where did the pastry box go? I can't talk with my mouth full."

No one answered her. Then she rolled her eyes and muttered, "I asked you to keep this between us but no," and picked up her purse to pull out a ring.

A ring with a nice diamond that reflected light in a sparkling rainbow and drew excited gasps. Only Tammy seemed unsurprised. When the round of congratulations and happy squeals died, Andi slipped it on her finger. "Really slows down my knitting." She sighed. "But I imagine I can adjust."

Edna pulled her hand closer so she could peer at the diamond. "Why weren't you wearing this, Andrea Jackson? It's beautiful."

"I needed to get used to the idea. Plus, I thought you could give the story more flair if I made a grand spectacle." She waggled her fingers. "This time, I want you to tell the story far and wide. Spread the news. Mark Taylor is going to be a married man. And his soon-to-be wife carries a gun. It's legal and everything." She smiled at Edna. "Did you get all that?"

Edna tsked and wrapped her arm around Andi's neck. The amazed look on Andi's face was as funny as anything she'd said that morning. Before the celebration died down, Elaine opened the door and left quietly.

In case anyone was looking out the window, she waved as she passed to show she didn't have a care in the world.

And she didn't, really.

Just because Andi's ring and their celebration made her feel lonely all over again didn't mean she had a good reason for getting emotional.

She had a bag full of yarn, a new hobby and a suggestion on how to spruce up her plans for the Bluebird. All in all, it had been a pleasant morning.

Her trouble with knitting had been disappointing. She'd expected to sit, pick up the needles and have everyone oohing over her natural ability. She should have tried studying in secret first, like her mother.

As if she had time for that.

But no one, not even Edna, had made her feel like a failure. She just needed practice. Lots of people needed practice to learn new things. And they'd laughed along with her. That made a difference.

Tall Pines was her home. Finding herself a new group of friends was a bonus to her strategy. A smile bubbled up when she remembered Tammy's invitation to return.

She would find the time to visit again. The next lesson could be the one that made all the difference.

After dropping said bag of yarn in the passenger seat, she turned as Edna said, "Sneaking away? That doesn't seem like you."

"I have a full agenda," Elaine answered, feeling her cheeks flush. If only she'd moved a bit faster. "Besides, you guys have a great reason to celebrate. I'll be back next Saturday, ready to make all kinds of knots again."

The two of them stared at each other, each one daring the other to say whatever it was she was really thinking.

Never one to back down from a challenge, Elaine said, "That's a nice tracksuit. Did you happen to get it on sale?" Then she smiled sweetly.

Edna ran a hand down her hip. "Yes, I did." Then she narrowed her eyes. "And it fits me perfectly. Puts a new swing in my step."

Elaine crossed her arms over her chest and waited for Edna to acknowledge her good advice.

Instead, Edna cleared her throat. "I wanted you to know that I was listening." She looked up and down the sidewalk to make sure no one else was eavesdropping on their showdown. "I liked what you said about families. If I were you…" She paused and rocked forward and back on her toes as if she was weighing her answer. "Well, don't forget the dads. Maybe fishing isn't a bad idea. Vacations take a lot of money. Why not offer something for everyone, make writing that check easier." Then she turned on the heel of her bright white sneaker and disappeared around the corner.

"Don't forget the dads." Elaine slid behind the steering wheel and buckled her seat belt.

It was sound advice.

She had no idea what to do with it, but she had a few days to figure it out. And since she was behind on the planning, thanks to her uncertainty over what was best for the new Bluebird and Tall Pines, she could even start at square one.

Before she could pull out into traffic, her phone rang. When she saw her father's number on the display, she considered letting it go to voice mail. She loved her father, but they had so little in common anymore.

Still, Elaine hadn't quite given up on hope.

"Hi, Dad." She flipped up the air conditioner and sighed at the blast of cold air.

"Elaine, how are you?" They made the usual small talk that began with the weather, went through his busy law practice and a cursory question-and-answer about her own clinic that always included how many patients she'd seen, how many shifts she was working and when she thought she'd be moving to a town with a real hospital or a real country club at the very least.

And as always, she said, "I'm happy in Tall Pines. It's home."

The silence stretched for a long minute, and she could almost hear her father's opinion of being happy in a town like Tall Pines. "Dad, what drew you to the Bluebird? When we took our vacations here, what made you want to stay?" He never fished much any other time of year, but while they were there, he went out every day in a borrowed boat.

"There was lots of room to spread out. Your mother was occupied so I could finally breathe, and I had plenty of time to myself, too." He covered the phone with a hand to answer some important question. Elaine was glad the conversation was muffled. She really didn't want to know. "Why do you ask?"

"It's nothing," Elaine said. She pressed her lips together and ignored the ache in her stomach. If her father hadn't changed, she hadn't, either. Getting her hopes up was still too easy. She remembered trailing behind him as often as she could, but they'd never fished together. Telling him about the opportunity she had to buy the inn would be an excellent chance to invite him to come and teach her.

If she'd felt more certain of her chances of winning, she would have done it, too. Invited him and his family to stay in return for a fishing lesson. She wasn't sure he'd agree this was a good decision and if she lost, he'd be disappointed whether he supported her choice or not. Better to sit on the news for now.

"Well, the reason I'm calling is Pete's decided he wants to try medical school. He's collecting applications." Her father huffed an impatient sigh. "I'm all for it, although my second son better choose law school." He'd never expected his daughter to. "So far his choice is UT Southwestern in Dallas. I've explained to him that it's a fine school, but he might want to aim higher, perhaps even Harvard or Stanford. Maybe you could talk to him."

Since she'd attended UT Southwestern and paid for it with very little help from her father, she had some strong opinions, none of which he'd appreciate. "Dad, UT is one of the top programs in the country. Pete would be lucky to be accepted."

Once Pete got his education, she wouldn't be getting phone calls for every cough, fever or new diagnosis. That meant she'd have even less contact with her father, the one who insisted his son's medical degree come with the finest brand name and a price tag to match.

Someday she'd learn to be completely fine with that.

"I'll have him call you anyway. Give him some advice, things to help with admissions." Before she could agree or disagree, her father ended the call.

Abrupt endings were something else she'd eventually adjust to.

Maybe.

So her dad had visited the Bluebird because it gave him plenty of space to get away from his family, not exactly the answer she'd been looking for but not really surprising. As she made the quick drive to the inn, she thought about hiring fishing guides.

A guide could teach her everything she needed to know about fishing.

But was fishing the best way to go? Maybe all the dads really needed was someplace to disappear to.

She bumped along the ruts and parked in her normal spot. Braving a quick glance toward the roof, she was relieved to see that Dean was not currently hanging upside down with a paintbrush in his hand.

His Jeep was missing, too.

She sat there longer than she meant to, staring out the windshield while she thought about her father's call. Talking to her mother would give her an excellent chance to complain long and loud but would only reinforce her mother's anger.

While venting would feel so, so good, it wouldn't fix anything.

That was the part that made her so sad. Nothing she did or said would transform her family back to the way she wanted it.

"Get out of the car, Elaine. Obsessing won't make you feel better," she said to herself.

As she walked up to the porch, she saw that Dean had finished painting the front of the inn completely. She leaned over the railing to gauge his progress. "Nearly done with this side." All that was left was the lowest quarter, a height comfortable for someone standing on the ground.

To confirm her suspicion that he was saving the last bit for her, she walked around to the back to see the same situation. Bright white paint covered the top three-quarters, leaving enough work for her to finish up.

"That will drive me crazy until it's finished." Elaine went inside and put on her painting shorts, relieved to have something to focus on other than her emotions. Determined to finish before he had a chance to crow, she hurried into the kitchen to grab some water, a necessity on a day as hot as today.

There, sitting on the crooked cabinet, was Dean's laptop. The screen displayed a photo of a vibrant blue flower. It sort of looked like the wildflower she'd taken her first shot of that morning.

"He must have stopped on the way down to take this." She surveyed the crisp detail of the petals and the hazy greens of the leaves and grass that faded into a perfect backdrop, one that gave dimension without distracting the eye from the star of the show. "Gorgeous."

She checked over her shoulder as if he might spring out from behind the door and then decided maybe it wouldn't hurt if she took a closer look.

"Really, he shouldn't leave it out if it's top secret." Curious to see what other shots he'd taken while she'd been exploring the world from behind her own camera, she tapped the touchpad to see if the photo was a part of a slideshow. What came up was a document outlining Dean's plan.

She scanned the list, wondering again if she should be seeing this. It was a lot more thorough than she'd expected. He'd left room for estimated costs and had the outline of a rough budget down the side. The marina was there, as well, with a five-year estimate of sales. At the bottom was a note about Phase Three.

Right now her plan had only two parts: renovate and reopen. She paced back and forth in front of the laptop, one hand covering her mouth. Why hadn't she realized just how far ahead of her he was? She had zero experience at playing catchup.

The bold heading "Return on Investment" caught her eye again. His plan was impressive. And she hated it. She'd been counting on Dean being less thorough than she was.

"Find what you were looking for?"

Elaine gasped and fumbled the water bottle that had lured her into the kitchen in the first place. She watched it roll down the counter and come to a stop while she tried to calm her heart. "You scared me."

"That was sort of the point." Dean stopped next to her and set two gallons of paint on the counter. "I hope I got the right color of blue."

No matter how desperately she wanted to say something lighthearted that would make him laugh and give her a shot at a quick getaway, Elaine's mind was a blank. "Sorry. I saw the picture. I thought I'd see what else you took this morning. That's all."

"You came for the photos, but stayed for the snooping." Dean crossed his arms over his chest. "Guess I can see that. At least you thought it was impressive. Loan officer at the First National Bank agreed."

He'd already met with someone at the bank? The sensation of falling even further behind made her knees weaken.

Get it together, Elaine. All you have to do is pretend nothing happened. Get a move on and don't look back.

She picked up the water bottle. "If you think I'm going to finish the job you left half-done, you're crazy. I've got to get some lists together for the contractor." And she had to make an appointment at the bank and then spend every free minute focused on her plan. That would mean less time with Dean. Win-win.

Ready to bluster her way out of danger, she moved toward the exit.

He stepped in front of her. "No, we need to talk first."

She had two options here. She could apologize again or attack, blame him for leaving his stuff all over until he was glad to see the back of her. Before she could commit to either strategy, he moved close enough that she could see the golden flecks in his eyes, and all she could do was concentrate on taking a deep breath and letting it go slowly while she waited for him to move away.

CHAPTER ELEVEN

"HAVE A PRODUCTIVE trip to town?" Dean asked as he watched Elaine fidget. "I thought I saw your car when I stopped at King's to get the paint. Where was that?" He tapped his chin. "Oh, yeah. I remember. Right around the corner from Purl's Place, a shop Edna happens to frequent on Saturdays. She told me she needed the first installment of my most exciting stories no later than Friday afternoon."

He propped his hands on his hips. "Hear any valuable gossip?"

The flush of color in her cheeks surprised him. He hadn't expected anything to embarrass Dr. Elaine Watson, and certainly nothing she undertook to win a competition.

"Andi's engaged." One shoulder jerked awkwardly in what he guessed was a shrug. "And I believe Edna's in love with you."

"She loves what I can do for her anyway. And that works for me. No luck in winning her over?" Of course not. He wasn't worried about losing his hand-picked judge. Coming up with stories to keep her satisfied without stirring up too much emotion had gotten easier each time they talked. She was the brains behind this operation, and if one thing had become clear the minute he sat across from Edna at the Country Kitchen, it was that she wanted to win nearly as much as Elaine did.

"She did give me some helpful advice." Elaine raised her eyebrows, and he was glad to see she hadn't yet conceded. "Once I talk it through with Jackie, I'm pretty sure it could be the piece I need to push me over the top."

She peeked over his shoulder as if she was trying to find an escape route. He reached around her to tap the touchpad on his laptop. If she wanted to go, one shoulder bump would clear the path. He waited to see what she would do.

"Not a big believer in personal space, Dean?" She inched sideways, closer to freedom, but she didn't make a break for it.

"Just curious about what sort of snooping you were doing." He frowned. "Does it count as industrial espionage if it involves a bed-and-breakfast?" He pretended to consider the question seriously. "Hospitality espionage?"

She shook her head, her lips twitching. When she didn't splutter out a defense, he smiled.

All was fair in love and war, after all.

And this was war. Absolutely.

Funny kind of war, genius.

"I was admiring your work."

"Yeah, my plans are awesome now. That Edna is a menace in more ways than one, but she does not play when it comes to business plans and world domination. In her mind, we're building the first link in a chain of fishing resorts." Remembering the stack of research she showed up with at their first lunch and the way the loan officer at the bank had kissed her cheek made him shake his head all over again. "She plots in terms of the big picture."

"That goes right along with her advice to me." Elaine finally met his stare. "I've been dreaming too small."

This close he could see the spark of inspiration in her bright eyes. Dean suddenly realized he was staring at her. Needing to shake the sensation that the rest of the world had disappeared, Dean motioned at the computer. "What did you think of the photo? Pretty good, huh?"

She looked at the picture again, glancing over her shoulder. "It is. When did you take it?"

"I didn't. That's your shot. Don't you recognize it?" He put his hands on her shoulders and urged her to turn then took a deep breath. "Here. Look." He clicked on the folder, opened the slideshow and advanced the shots. "Some of them are…"

"Not good!" she said, laughing at a blurry shot of what he thought was a knothole in tree bark.

"The problem with that one is the exposure." He reached around her and felt her tense against him. "If we change it to black-and-white, adjust the exposure and color balance, then all you see is texture." When the photo converted he eased back and told himself to get out of the kitchen.

"And that's exactly what I was going

for," she murmured as she flipped through the rest of the pictures. "Not bad for my first lesson, right?"

He shifted away to lean against the counter. "You don't sound surprised. I wasn't, either. I'm guessing there are few things you don't do well."

She closed the slideshow and straightened. "I have a snarl of yarn that says there's at least one thing I don't do well." She grimaced. "My cover story for entering Purl's Place was a knitting lesson. Either the instructions were less than effective or I've met my match. I would say I went down in flames, but the shop is still standing."

"Most people aren't experts at everything they try," he said. "That's normal."

She frowned. Elaine might not expect everyone else to be perfect, but she had seriously high standards for herself. He was considering pointing that out when her phone rang.

"Hi, Mom," Elaine said. Her smile as she answered this call was real, not like the pained one he'd seen the last time her mother called. He wondered what had changed.

"Are you all packed up?" Elaine reached to pick up her water bottle, and Dean considered bowing out. Unfortunately, he hadn't had his chance to really torment her about snooping on his laptop.

"You met a guy in your cooking class." Elaine's shoulders slumped, and the energy that made her smile bright and beautiful faded. "So you aren't coming next week?"

Now he wished he'd made a quick exit, but she was pacing in front of the doorway, her shoulders set in a tense line. Whatever was coming would not be good.

"No, that's fine. Just…" Elaine swallowed hard. "I'll talk to you later."

Then she jammed the button to end the call, set the phone and water bottle down carefully and covered her face with both hands.

"Everything okay?" He winced at how loud his voice was, but her seething tension made him nervous.

"Just another something I don't do very well. Take care of my mother." She resumed pacing, this time slowly like she was lost and trying to find the right direction. "If she were my patient, and I gave her the same advice—life-saving advice— over and over and she ignored me every single time and kept coming in with broken bones, I would ask her to find a new doctor. Maybe. I don't know. But she's my mother. She does the same thing again and again and then collapses with every broken heart. It's ridiculous."

And disappointing. That was clear. He could see frustration and sadness tangled up in her tight lips and sad eyes.

She'd also had a lot of experience dealing with the mix. She straightened her shoulders and pasted on a smile. "And I should have learned not to expect so much from her. I thought we were on a good track, planning this trip to Tall Pines. Then she did what she always does. Why wouldn't I expect this?"

Dean glanced awkwardly around the room, desperate for something to cheer her up. Why? He had no idea. He hated to see the bitter disappointment on her face when moments before she'd been so happy.

"And why am I unloading all this on

you?" She rolled her eyes. "Sorry. I apologize for snooping. I should know better. I do know better. I saw the photo and couldn't resist. Then I saw the plans and I could tell I needed to catch up. They're really good. Thorough."

"Thanks." What a weak answer. It did nothing to make her smile genuine or even to keep the conversation moving. But it was the only answer he had.

She held up one finger. "But I'm not afraid of a come-from-behind win. Remember our jog?"

The contest she'd won when he didn't know they were racing. He could say that. Pick up the trash talk, get things back to normal between them again. She was making it easy.

But he might never have another chance to talk to her honestly about something that obviously bothered her.

Dean had handled a lot of things on his own for too long. Thanks to this place and her, he was beginning to understand that alone wasn't the best way to endure.

"So she's not coming to visit?"

Elaine glanced at the doorway and

then looked up to study the ceiling, another surface that could stand some fresh white paint. "She can't be alone. She goes through one grand love that dies in flames and then suffers until the next come along. That means lots of phone calls where I give sound, helpful advice. Take a class. Find a job. Come and visit. I thought she might actually take it this time and make a change."

"That's got to be disappointing." He couldn't imagine a lifetime of picking up the pieces, going through all the highs and lows of failed relationships from the front-row seat.

His father's slow meltdown had been nearly impossible for him to understand as a kid. He'd wanted to rage and fight when his mother died. His father had folded, shut down.

But at least he hadn't made a habit of it.

And losing a wife to cancer had to be a sound reason for a meltdown. Now that he'd gained some maturity, he could see he'd had his own emotional storm, not a bit better than his father's. Did Elaine understand she was still going through her storm?

"Disappointing? I don't know. It's exhausting is what it is. I should pull back, let her figure it out by herself. For my own good, I should tell her to stop calling with her relationship news." She squeezed her eyes closed. "But she's the one who always shows up for me. Always."

Dean stepped closer and before he could figure out what he wanted to do, he wrapped his arms around her shoulders and pulled her closer. "You can't sit back and watch her hurt…because you're you."

Instead of pushing him away, she rested her head against his shoulder and tangled her fists in his loose T-shirt, as if she was afraid he'd desert her before she was ready. He closed his eyes and rested his chin on her head. Then they stood there in the ugly kitchen in a complete moment of connection.

"When I asked my dad why he didn't tell me about his heart trouble, he said that he didn't want to watch me worry." Dean paused, wondering if he should shut up. He wasn't a doctor, didn't spend all day trying to cure patients. There was a good chance he'd say exactly the wrong thing.

"So I should…what? Keep doing what I'm doing?" She didn't look up at him, just stepped closer, and he held her more tightly.

"Well, I was thinking… I would rather he'd been honest with me. If that had turned into something more serious, fatal, and I never knew until it was too late, I might have thought he didn't care." Dean squeezed his eyes shut and willed the tears burning his nose to disappear. He had to take this vulnerability thing in stages.

"But he cared so much he didn't want to see you hurt." Her tired sigh breezed over his nape, and he fought the urge to shiver. "I see where you're going with this."

That was a good thing because he'd almost lost track of the plan the minute she'd stepped closer.

"I should be honest about how I feel. Blaming her for not making a change is unfair when she doesn't even get that it's hurting me." She smoothed the wrinkles in his shirt. "You're pretty smart for a guy who hangs upside down off the roof for fun."

He laughed, relieved that whatever murky thought he'd managed to express had helped her find some comfort. She made him sound a lot smarter than he really was.

That was a truly impressive skill to find in a beautiful woman. "You're being awfully nice to someone who's been snooping through your stuff." She tilted her head back to look up at him. "You must lack the killer instinct. Are you okay with losing?" Her small smile was a challenge.

One he couldn't resist. He closed the distance between them and pressed his lips to hers. She gave a small gasp, but instead of moving away, she returned his kiss, each slide of her lips over his a shock to his system. For that brief moment, nothing else mattered, not the Bluebird or winning or losing or her mother or his father or whatever came next. Her sweet lips and the way she fit against him changed everything.

But only for a second.

Then she eased back, met his gaze and said, "What a bad idea."

Nothing like crashing to earth to bring a man back to the real world.

He pointed at the paint can. "I'll be outside, working on shutters." And then he turned and made a quick exit.

Until he realized he'd need the paint can. When he forced himself back into the kitchen, she had braced one hand against the counter they'd worked to rehang, the other hand pressed against her lips.

He didn't ask if she was okay. He didn't force her to explain herself, mainly because he knew exactly what she meant. And he didn't make a case for more kisses. He didn't have to. That one had been so good, it should speak for itself.

He grabbed the paint can and did a countdown of how much longer they had until the bet was decided.

Because the next day, the one right after the judges made their decision, he was going to figure out what to do about the doctor.

CHAPTER TWELVE

EVER SINCE THE KISS, she'd managed to avoid Dean. If he was on a ladder working on the shutters, she was inside making measurements and lists. When he went back to paint the spots he'd left for her, she researched all the hotels in the area, hoping to find the key to winning in their lists of amenities. And he worked without complaining.

If he was sitting on the end of the dock, she was staring out the window of her bedroom, finding her gaze drawn to him.

It was enough to make her feel as if she was either very good or very bad at stalking him. There wasn't much in between.

"Stupid yarn. Do what I tell you." She forced herself to stretch and then rewrap the yarn around the needle a little more loosely. Knitting was more fun when it didn't require a feat of strength to get every stitch off the needle.

Or so she imagined. She hadn't quite gotten the hang of it.

But she'd decided knitting might help her think about something other than Dean, losing the Bluebird or the kiss. The three of them together were too much, and each one separately was enough to distract her from whatever she was doing.

Wondering if he deserved to win made it even more difficult to build her plan. A niggling voice whispered maybe it was more important for him to keep his home than for her to be proven right again, leaving her fingers frozen on the keyboard.

When her phone rang, she set the needles down with a tiny bit of relief. "Hi, Mom."

"Are you busy? I forgot what days you're working at the after-hours emergency clinic this week." Her mother's voice was clear, steady.

"I asked to go to one shift, so it'll be Thursday evenings from now on. My practice has kept me busy enough lately that I've been considering eliminating the once-a-month Saturday hours, too." Elaine propped her feet up on the freshly scraped railing and tried to relax. "But so many working parents need those appointments."

"I hope your schedule will settle down. It's hard to make plans when your shifts are up in the air like that."

Elaine frowned at the phone. Everything her mother said was true, but it was unusual to hear her say something so businesslike about her job. Usually her mother's comments had to do with how impossible it was to date doctors.

"How did the final class go? Did you wow everyone with your soufflé?" She would not ask about the guy, whoever he was. Chances were he'd be gone before she had to meet him at a holiday dinner. "My mother, the head of the class, right?"

"It fell. Not only did it fall, but the crater in the center looked like an area you might find alien life. It was ugly, but it was a lot of fun to try. I'm definitely going to bake it again." The laugh that accompanied her mom's declaration lifted Elaine's spirits. It was hard to stay mad at her mother. That was a good thing.

Dean passed the porch on his way to wash out his paintbrush without glancing at her. She couldn't decide if he was embarrassed by the kiss or mad about her reaction. Could be both.

His advice had been floating to the surface now and then, and since they were both in a good mood, Elaine decided to go for it. "Mom, I needed to let you know how…disappointed I am that you aren't coming for a visit." There. She'd done it.

Her mother cleared her throat. "Well… I'm not sure what to say, Elaine." The silence stretched across the phone line. "You're always so busy. I didn't think you'd miss me at all."

The words hit with enough force to make Elaine catch her breath. "I… Of course I miss you. I wanted to share this place with you, the one we loved so much. Both of us. I asked you to come, remember?" How could her mother misunderstand that?

"I didn't want to be an imposition." Her mother sighed. "You have an important career. Just like your father. I understand that spending time on a visit is a sacrifice. Besides, I'm happy enough here." The tone of her voice didn't match her words.

Was Elaine as distant as her father? Just

as hard to know and love? She rubbed her forehead with cold fingers and tried to avoid squirming in the noisy chair.

All these years, she'd been strong. That hadn't been easy. She'd also been impatient and judgmental and too smart for her own good.

If she didn't make a change, find something else besides her work, she'd regret it. Someday she might have a daughter she didn't know and couldn't talk to just like her father did.

He loved his job. He was good at it. Did he think it was easier to stick with what he was good at—talking shop—rather than face the prospect of failing?

"Mom, I'm sorry I've made you feel that way. Please come for a visit. I would enjoy it so much." And if it was after the Bluebird decision and if she didn't win the day, she'd beg Robert Collins for a special guest pass, pack up her own tea and they'd have a special afternoon just the two of them.

"I keep thinking I will, Elaine, but…" Elaine gripped the phone so tightly her fingers ached. "Then I decide I'll wait until I'm more…together. Like you. With everything going right." Her mother laughed. "I did take some of your advice. I got a part-time job selling kitchenware, of all things. This cooking class has warped my brain."

Until Jerry, the last husband who desired the perfect hostess, not a content wife, her mother had always volunteered and worked sales jobs because they made her happy. She enjoyed working with people.

"That's great, Mom. When you can get a couple of days off, you and…what was his name?" Elaine waited, aware that she was about to torpedo her own daydreams by including the new boyfriend but prepared to do whatever it took to convince her mother to come.

"Stephen, but forget about him." Her mother cleared her throat again. "I've decided I'm not ready to date. When I am, another Stephen will come along."

Elaine sighed and stretched the tight muscles in her legs. Her knuckles were white until she flexed her hand to ease the tension. "That's really healthy for you. Learn this job you love, then figure out what you want next."

"I'm sorry I let you down, Elaine." Her mother's voice was hard to hear.

"It's just a trip. We'll reschedule." Elaine had to clear her throat. "But I do miss you, so let's make it soon, okay?"

"When's the big decision?"

"We're waiting for Robert's return. I've got a few estimates still to come from the contractor. I met with the loan officer at the bank yesterday, so I'm close. I need to come up with…something new, something killer to attract male guests. Jackie, my partner in this contest, mentioned hiring guides for the lake. Maybe that's the best solution." Elaine craned her neck to make sure Dean was far, far away.

Her solution was very close to his whole reason for being, another thing that bothered her.

"Make sure you have plenty of family activities. I remember you trailing after your father, his tiny shadow. He couldn't shake you, could he?" her mother asked, a smile in her voice. "I blame him for the dried leaf scrapbook to this day."

Let it go, Elaine. You've already come out of one battle unbloodied.

But today was apparently the day to right old hurts.

"You should blame Mrs. Hopkins, my third-grade teacher. She's the one who made me love science. Neither one of my parents encouraged it, that's for sure." When her teeth snapped shut to keep more angry words from escaping, Elaine relaxed her grip on the phone. "And that's why I have this fabulous career, the one I worked so hard for."

"Maybe you're right. You did what you loved anyway. I'm so proud of you." When her mother said it, more often Elaine could hear "But I don't understand you at all."

This time, she knew it was still true. She and her mother would always be different, but that hadn't changed the fact that Elaine needed her.

Her mother's love didn't depend on the things they had in common. Her mother just loved her. Period. Always had, always would. Whether Elaine was head of the class or a selfish overachiever with too little time for what mattered, her mother was her biggest fan.

The lump in her throat was hard to ignore. Elaine tried to imagine what it might be like to live without that love, how hard it would be to lose her mother, and wondered where Dean was.

"Well, think about rescheduling the trip, Mom. After next week, I'll have an inn at my disposal or you'll be sleeping on my couch in my cramped apartment, but either way, it'll be wonderful to see you." She picked up the knitting needles again. "Maybe I can take you to Purl's Place for a knitting lesson."

She ended the call on her mother's disbelieving laugh and started the chair rocking, the rhythmic creak a little faster than true relaxation but comforting anyway. Knitting might keep the tears away.

"Do you approve of the paint?" Dean asked from the yard. He pointed at the shutters along the side. "Good match?"

To get more time to put herself together, Elaine leaned over the railing to see bright blue shutters against the crisp white paint.

"Wonderful. Matches the bluebirds." She considered the nesting boxes and reminded herself to get on with her improvement plans. She'd stalled lately, and Dean was surging ahead, but now that she was close on her proposal, she could tackle new projects. "I've been researching how to attract more bluebirds. I'm going to clear out the garden then maybe go into town, see if Mr. King will order some mealworms." The grimace that followed her plan was uncontrollable. She hadn't fully committed to putting out the worms, but getting the bluebirds back seemed important enough to overcome her small amount of distaste. "Suet doesn't seem to have been the magic meal."

"It would be nice to have some bluebirds," Dean said.

The awkward silence stretched out between them until she cleared her throat. "I don't suppose you have time for a small project. I've been thinking about painting the nesting boxes." She shivered. "But I'd need a *ladder*."

Dean studied the boxes for a minute. "So, basically, I'll be the one with the project. Not you."

Uncomfortable at the reminder of how much work he'd done around the Bluebird compared with what she'd managed, Elaine put her mangled knitting in the Purl's Place bag at her feet and stood. "You're right. Never mind. I can do this on my own." But she really didn't want to.

His heavy sigh stopped her in her tracks. "No, these are important. I'll help."

She thought about arguing with him, insisting she could handle it all, but decided against it.

By the time she'd grabbed a clean brush and the leftover white paint, Dean was staring up at the first nesting box.

He took the can and the brush from her. "You know, painting leaves plenty of time for thinking." He carefully cut in around the bottom of the box and along the edges before covering all four sides with white paint. "Every one of these projects I do for you or with you helps you win the bet. Not me."

He didn't look at her as he shifted to the next box. "That part of your plan?"

"Um, well…" Elaine rubbed her nose. "Only indirectly. That's why I started the projects. Today I wanted to talk to you."

He frowned and stared into the distance before he shook his head. Neither one of them said anything else while he methodically worked through all the nesting boxes. "Bring the blue paint for the roofs." Something about his tone gave her the old feeling of uncertainty and unease that her father had always been able to call up. He was disappointed.

She handed him the second can of paint and admired how fresh and clean the new nesting boxes were. Surely the birds would return to such beautiful homes.

"For someone who wanted to talk, you haven't said much." He stared hard at the brush he was rinsing.

That was a good point. Elaine shoved her hands into her pockets and tried to figure out what to say.

After he turned the water off, he studied her face and sighed. "When I chose the paint for the shutters, I was actually trying to match the morning glories that used to trail up the fence post over there." He pointed to the far side of the garden. "I hadn't thought of them in a while, not until you reminded me what they were called. Now I can remember my mother babying the vines and crowing in happiness when they bloomed." He studied the empty spot where morning glories should be. "She was always so patient, more optimistic than anyone I've ever met, even with cancer."

"If the vines don't come back, we'll put out seed next year. This place should have morning glories, too." After the phone call with her mother and the reminder of all the moments Dean had missed with Martha Collins, Elaine ached, her raw emotions hard to control.

When she wrapped her arms around Dean and squeezed as hard as she could, he hesitated before returning her hug. Neither of them said a word. Eventually, she forced herself to let go, suddenly aware of the tightness of the muscles across her shoulders, but she didn't step back. So many words tumbled in her head, lame attempts to say the right thing to make everything better. None of them would work.

But she couldn't stand this distance. She'd stopped seeing him as an opponent. In a short time, Dean had become someone who understood her better than just about anyone in the world. She didn't want to lose that, not over the Bluebird. And not over a kiss.

"I took your advice. I explained to my mother how it felt to be dropped for another guy." She closed her eyes, pressed her forehead to his shoulder. "Maybe something will change. I hope so."

When Dean ran his hands down her back, she opened her eyes to watch him. If the world could just stop, right here, she'd be content. His small frown made sense, but he hadn't pushed her away.

"I hope so, too. If she comes, this is a good spot to heal old wounds." He stepped back and climbed the stairs to the porch. "I can't believe I said that. I mean, I don't have any old wounds, you know? I should be over my grief from so long ago."

"Some grief sticks with you." Elaine sighed and followed him. She didn't want to examine her issues anymore. She wanted to move on, something else she and Dean had in common.

"Are we going to talk about the kiss or keep dodging each other? And just now, that hug…" He leaned against the railing. "I'm confused. It's a big place. We could manage it for another week. I got a text from my dad saying he was heading in this direction by way of the Hoover Dam." He shook his head. "Words I never expected to say—*text from my dad*."

"I'm confused, too, but the hug… Sometimes it's too hard to put the way I feel into words." She closed her eyes. "Most of the time actually, but… Well, thank you, I guess, for the advice. I love my mother."

He blinked slowly. "What do I say? You're welcome?"

He had the strangest way of settling her. His confused frown made her smile.

"But the kiss… Either way, one of us is a winner, and the other one's a loser. Not the stuff of fairy tales."

"And what…you don't have time for losers? Winner that you are?" Dean crossed his arms over his chest. "Are you telling me good sportsmanship is a myth?"

"No, it's not a myth, but it's not really… natural, either. It's something we learn, we tell ourselves we should be good sports, but we really wish we'd won. On the inside, we're all bad sports." She dropped down in the rocking chair and sent it into motion.

"Dr. Elaine Watson, wrong about something. I should call Mark, see if he has room to print it on the front page." Dean braced his hands on the arms of her rocking chair. "Because you're wrong. Maybe it's only this one case, but if you win and I lose, I can be happy for you. I understand what you want. My mother would love to see her home restored, even if it hurts me to imagine the Bluebird without her. If you win, I'll congratulate you."

Speechless, she stared into his dark eyes. His commitment to every word he said was clear. He refused to let her look away.

She believed him.

"You'd stay here in Tall Pines? Without the Bluebird, you'd build a new home here?" She wanted his answer to be yes. The town might never be the same without him, but how long would it be until he rolled on to the next hot spot?

And how would she feel if he did?

"I don't know. I can't imagine where I'd go, but..." Dean's words trailed off, and he turned to look out across the lake. "Wherever my camera takes me, I guess. Without the Bluebird, all I've really got is the job."

As nice as winning felt and as much as she wanted to call this home, would that be enough to make her happy if Dean left?

Why did the thought of him picking up where he'd left off, putting himself in danger to tell the stories that needed to be told, make it so hard to breathe?

Was that love? And if it was, shouldn't she…drop out of this silly competition?

The Bluebird could hold him here, keep him safe. She knew it in her heart.

He needed this place more than she did.

But she couldn't lose.

Don't be silly, Elaine. Whether he stays or goes, you need to do whatever it takes to make yourself happy. You love the Bluebird. Let the chips fall where they may. Men can come and go, but the Bluebird is solid.

If her happiness depended on whatever Dean Collins decided, she was letting herself down.

But forgetting all that to kiss him would be so easy. He was so close and warm. The understanding and affection she could see in his eyes made him seem a safe bet, something she'd never found before.

Dean stepped back. "That yarn you're mangling, have the ladies at Purl's Place seen it?"

Elaine fought the urge to pull him closer, to hold on to their connection. She stared at him until she remembered he'd asked her a question.

"Not yet. I'm practicing so the next time I go, they'll be amazed at my progress and assume I've got the touch." She held up the zigzag swatch that was supposed to be a neat rectangle of regular stitches. There were no holes, but she'd somehow knit three knots in. "I have a long way to go, as you can see."

"What would happen if you weren't the best knitter in town, but you went anyway just for fun?"

Elaine tried to come up with a good answer. There wasn't one. "If I can't get the hang of this, I won't go. Of course not." What a crazy suggestion. Why spend time and, in this case, money, doing something she was no good at? If she didn't get the hang of it this week, she'd toss in the needles. Maybe buy a camera. She almost asked him for a recommendation.

They might not be friends after Robert returned. Worse, Dean might not even be here anymore.

That thought was what kept her on edge, the fear of watching him walk away when he lost. The needles slipped from her fingers, and she scrambled to keep the yarn from escaping.

"You know, I'm not the best fisherman. Neither is my dad. I fall so often when I hike that every pair of jeans I own has a rip." He shrugged. "That doesn't mean I don't enjoy almost every minute."

"But you could be doing things you're really good at." Like kissing. "Wouldn't that be a better use of your time?"

"To improve the world? Maybe. To enjoy this life, I really don't believe so. It's good to make mistakes. Sometimes they're a lot of fun." He winked. "Besides that, most mere mortals need practice to be proficient. You might not be a world-class knitter, but you could have a hobby you love if you can put up with being bad at it for a while." He leaned forward. "Did I blow your mind?"

Her lips were twitching, but she fought off the smile. He was so cute sometimes.

It was unfair. And honestly, this was why she needed him.

Maybe enough to actually hope she lost this competition.

"I'm headed into town to meet up with Edna for some homestretch fine tuning." He grimaced. "Why does that sound painful?"

"I have a meeting with Nick to talk about the final estimates. Then it's all over but the judging. And I'm ready." She shrugged. "More time for my knitting."

He trotted down the steps to stop in the shady yard. "Consider your plan B, Doc. I know I'm going to win just like I know your plan is solid and would work against anyone other than me." He looked at the keys in his hand. "That doesn't mean I want you to lose. I sure don't want it to mean we're friendly enemies." He looked up again. "I want to believe I could still call you when the night gets bad. More than that, I think we can get over winners and losers and just be us, two people who love this place and who have a lot in common."

He pointed his finger at her. "Plus, we kiss really well."

Before she could answer—and say what, exactly—he was gone, bumping down the track to town.

And she was sitting on the porch with only her bad knitting to keep her company.

There were worse places to be.

Before the kiss, she might have been happy to see the last of him. Now her single chair creaking sounded lonelier than ever.

CHAPTER THIRTEEN

A WEEK LATER, Elaine sat across from the contractor, Nick, and Jackie, the drawings and budget spread out across her desk.

"Thanks for coming by after the office closed. During the day we'd never have enough time." She ran a finger down the figures on the budget, hoping any holes would jump out at her. Unfortunately, her heart wasn't in it, and her brain had followed her heart.

This is it, Elaine. You can win this. Pay attention.

"I checked with King. The bathroom tiles you picked online can be ordered and delivered, no problem." Nick pointed at the sketch he'd made of the thoroughly modernized kitchen. "And we'll have the flooring in less than a week after we order, so when we finish demo, we should be ready to start with the floor."

She smiled at him. "Thanks for all your help, Nick. I'm sure I've made things complicated."

He waved away her thanks. "Nah, it's all part of the job. Some people just won't accept a professional opinion. You had to search out your own sources, and I can't blame you."

Jackie cleared his throat, so Elaine turned to him. "These figures are good," she said. "It'll help to know how many visitors came to the area when the Bluebird was open."

He put both elbows on the chair's armrests. "I thought so, too. And don't forget the list of fishing guides. Good idea to show that with your plan, we can have a place women and men will enjoy. Can't see how we can lose, Doc." His superior glance in Nick's direction might have made her laugh, but she was sure Jackie would not appreciate that.

She hoped Jackie was right, but if there was ever a competition she was less certain of winning, she couldn't remember it.

"I've seen what Edna and Dean came up with so we've got some stiff competition, but you've been a big help." She offered both men her hand and managed not to wince when Jackie squeezed it tightly. "Thank you for your help, Jackie."

He popped up from the chair, ready to march off. A lot of people thought Jackie was a busybody, a man who was far too quick to file a lawsuit. Working with him proved to Elaine that he also had a shrewd brain and a vested interest in the success of businesses in Tall Pines. Jackie made a much better friend than enemy.

"Remember our deal. When you win, no meals at the inn but plenty of Country Kitchen menus scattered around." Before she could agree or say a polite goodbye, he'd opened the door and disappeared.

The corners of Nick's mouth turned up as he accepted her handshake. "Jackie is an interesting little man." His bright blue eyes and lopsided smile made it impossible not to smile, no matter what was on the line. The jeans with small paint splotches and his too-long hair reminded her of Dean. "No matter who wins this, I'm really looking forward to getting my hands on that beautiful old building. The designs you chose bring enough modern updates to satisfy the choosiest guests but still fit the inn's style. You're good at this."

"You've been a big help," Elaine said.

"I hope we continue working together." Nick left, and she could hear him tell Nina goodbye as he walked out the front door. There was no doubt in her mind that he would do a fine job. But still...

How sad was it that this massive, satis-fying project felt so hollow without Dean as her partner?

No time to worry about that now.

"Guess I better have everything I need." She picked up all the papers, carefully ar-ranged them in the binder and closed it to stare at the photo of the newly painted inn. She'd borrowed a camera from Dean in a painfully polite exchange, snapped the photo and had Nina help her print it out.

In a move she tried to consider prudent instead of cowardly, she'd spent last night in her tiny apartment. The closer the dead-line got, the harder it was to trust herself. She had to win. Every daydream she had about her future featured the Bluebird.

But watching Dean leave and wonder-

.ing if he was safe would make enjoying that future difficult.

And the silly voice that whispered, "What if you can have it all?" scared her. Real life was never perfect. Winning and having Dean settle in Tall Pines were mutually exclusive outcomes.

And hoping to lose was so wrong, it gave her headaches.

She put her head on the binder and whispered a quick prayer that her efforts would be good enough. The weeks she'd spent at the bed-and-breakfast had proven to be some of the happiest she could remember. Even in the state it was in and with all the hard work. And even with Dean Collins around.

The Bluebird was where she was meant to be.

"Sleeping on the job, Dr. Watson?"

Elaine blinked as she straightened slowly. "Mom? What are you doing here?" She got a quick glimpse of pale pink linen, her mother's sleek blond bob and immaculately applied lipstick before her mother wrapped her arms around her neck in a hug. Instead of warning her about germs or asking any more questions, Elaine closed her arms around her mother and held on tight.

Nothing else mattered.

Her mom was here.

When she needed her most, her mother was here.

The sting of tears surprised her, and her mother stepped back, obviously taken off guard at the welcome. "Tears, Elaine?" Her mother knelt in front of her and wrapped both of Elaine's hands in hers. "What's happened? Did you lose?"

"Not yet, but I'm afraid I'm going to." She cleared her throat and forced a laugh. "Silly. A grown woman crying about a competition for the right to pour money into a run-down old building. I haven't even lost yet!"

If she told her mother she was even more afraid of winning, her mom would suspect an imposter. Neither one of them knew what to do with a confused Elaine. Setting goals and surpassing them was who she was, and that certainty was so much better than the confused cloud she'd been under for a week. Only seeing patients gave her any relief.

And she hadn't been on the verge of tears until her mother showed up. Maybe they were actually about something else, but it was easier to blame the Bluebird.

Her mother frowned and for a second Elaine thought she was going to ask a question or force the issue. Instead, she sighed. "You never have handled losing well. Remember the eighth-grade science fair?"

"My display on how light travels through air versus water should have won over Derek Parker's dumb rock identification display." Relieved to have a distraction, Elaine jumped into the old familiar conversation.

"You loved Derek Parker and rocks. He was the only boy who would have been impressed by your leaf collection, but you were probably mad you didn't think of doing rocks first." Her mother brushed the curls out of Elaine's eyes.

"Yes, but I did the leaf collection for fun. The science fair was about experimentation and growth." Elaine's lips twitched as she met her mother's amused stare. "Never mind about that. I'm so happy you're here." She hugged her mother again and her perfume, the faint scent of roses, was a comfort.

"This is a busy time for Bake and Take, so they need advance notice for any vacation. But I had to get some time off." Her mother grimaced as she stood up and held out a hand to stall Elaine's list of questions about her symptoms. "It's just old age combined with standing on my feet. Rest is all I need."

Biting her tongue on the offer to run a blood test to check for inflammation or arthritic markers, Elaine nodded and handed her the binder she'd worked so hard on. "Here. This is what I have."

Elaine tapped a pen on her legal pad and waited while her mother flipped slowly through the drawings and murmured what sounded like vaguely positive words now and then. "Fishing guides. Not a terrible idea. Your father never could find a fish."

Not that he'd been looking very hard. Elaine didn't even consider saying it out loud. Whatever new path her mother was on was promising.

Eventually, she closed the binder. "Nice shot. This is how I remember the Bluebird."

"Took some work to get it there." Elaine picked up the binder and shoved it in her tote. "And I took that shot. I'm dabbling with photography."

"The doctor taking her own advice," her mother said. "What will the world come to?"

Elaine grinned. "As of now, you and I are out of here. It's time to show off the Bluebird." They left the office, pausing to wave at Nina, who was just finishing up. "Follow me?" Elaine said.

Her mother nodded and slid behind the wheel of her old Mercedes. It was a gift from a boyfriend before Jerry that he'd never talked her into dumping. Her mother had good taste and a strong backbone when it came right down to it.

Elaine darted a few glances in the rearview mirror to make sure her mother stuck close all the way through town. Getting lost in Tall Pines wouldn't be easy, but it could be done, especially on a day like today where unwary tourists could wander out in the road.

As she passed Purl's Place, she saw the normal crowd seated in the window. She'd been looking forward to showing off her improved knitting, but she'd forgotten it was the first Saturday of the month. The office had long waiting lists for those special days, so she couldn't get out of it.

Next week she'd be able to really wow them. If she had time, she'd try some pre-study, maybe learn to purl all on her own.

Once she made the turn onto the dirt road, she could see that Dean had been busy again. Instead of ruts that threatened to make her car tumble nose-first into oblivion, there was a smooth surface with fresh gravel and neatly mown grass. The road looked like something out of a bucolic old postcard.

"Work a few shifts, sleep in your tiny apartment a night or two and the man makes miracles happen," she muttered and then rounded the curve in the road to see a giant RV blocking the view. "And Robert is home."

A shot of adrenaline boosted her heart rate. "You knew the clock was running out, Elaine. Relax. Do the best you can. Whatever happens will work out." Her calming lecture didn't make it easier to breathe, but parking sedately in her usual spot probably made it seem that she had everything under control.

"Wow. This place is almost as beautiful as I remember it." Her mother slung her purse over her shoulder and dragged a small suitcase behind her. Her voice wasn't as cheerful as it had been, but she forced a smile. "Well, except for the truly impressive travel rig blocking the view."

"Yeah, you got here just in time. Robert's home." Elaine shut the car door calmly and jumped when her mother wrapped her hand around Elaine's arm.

"Not to worry. As long as you've done your best, it will all work out." Her mother peered at her over the top of her sunglasses. "Trust your mother."

Like a flash, Elaine realized that she'd been living entirely too long with the cautious doubt that made her trust no one but herself. It was safer. Other people let her down but she'd never failed at something that was important.

If she didn't win and she couldn't take a

chance on another person, who would she believe in?

She wrapped her arms around her mother's neck again. "I don't know how you knew I needed you, but I won't ever forget this."

Her mother whispered, "Always so strong. I'm happy to help." When her mom eased back, she looked more grimly determined than joyful.

"Well, hello there! I was beginning to think you'd come to your senses," Robert Collins yelled from the shady front porch. Dean stood by his side, his arms crossed over a T-shirt covered in white and blue paint, the obvious advertisement for how he'd spent his free time the past few weeks.

Glad to have part of her own team for support, Elaine tucked her arm through her mother's, and they both walked slowly over the grass to the steps.

"No way, Mr. Collins. You know me. I never give up, not even with stubborn patients." Elaine glanced at Dean and then added, "This is my mother, Catherine Stillman. Mom, this is Robert Collins and his son, Dean."

Elaine eased back and watched her mother shake hands with both men. "What a lovely home you have here."

Robert nodded. "When I left, it was a wreck. I was certain Dean's plan to open a fish camp was the only option, but now I'm not so sure. Seems Dean and Elaine have been busy. Painting was a huge improvement." He leaned forward. "And they didn't even draw blood."

"Dr. Watson and I have done a decent job of getting along, Dad," Dean said quietly, his eyes meeting hers again.

"I never would have believed it, Doc. You did something to light the fire under him, no doubt. When I left, he was working his way up to a full day of sitting on the dock." Robert clapped his hand on his son's shoulder, but the teasing missed the mark for Dean. He frowned, a muscle twitching in his clenched jaw.

"Well, I've been impressed with how hard he's worked, Mr. Collins. This paint job… I could never have managed that." Somehow she couldn't avoid the truth even when it would be better to pile on more doubts.

"And she's been an effective prod, especially after she hung most of the cabinets by herself." Dean had one shoulder propped against the bright blue post.

"You did what?" her mother asked with a scandalized gasp. "What would make you think you should try a man's job, Elaine Watson?"

"Well, I'd already finished mowing the grass so..." She watched her mother's mouth open and close without making a sound.

Then she looked at Robert. "And a friend asked me to do him a favor, so I had to get along. No drawing blood. Imagine my shock when I realized how nice it was to work beside my opponent." Dean frowned at his father, who might have whistled an innocent tune except her mother interrupted. "A doctor. Doing manual labor. You always did have the strangest interests."

Robert clapped his hands in the tense silence. "Well, it's all worked out. Tomorrow we'll know who's going to lead the next phase of renovations. Can't wait to see what you've come up with."

"I'll call Jackie, see if we can meet at the

Country Kitchen for dinner or something," Dean said, watching her closely.

Her first thought was that it was perfect. If she lost, she didn't have to come back to the Bluebird in defeat. She could go right on home to her tiny apartment and lick her wounds in private.

Well, with her mother watching.

And that would mean she'd have to soldier through.

But if all the judges were here, they could see how much beauty was left at Spring Lake. Maybe they'd be less willing to change it all.

"Could we meet at the Bluebird? It'll be easier for the judges to see its potential." She could still be packed and prepared to drive away immediately if she lost, as long as she convinced her mother to be ready, too.

Was she really prepared to concede the war before the last battle was engaged? That was unacceptable.

"I'll call Jackie," Elaine said. "You line up Edna and…" They both turned to look at Robert. "Who's the third judge?"

"Ray Evans. Hope that's okay." He

glanced from Dean to her and back. "And I'll call all three, take care of this. Plus, the newspaper man wants to come out, do a story on the whole thing. Could be a nice start on the publicity we'll need when we reopen. I'm anxious to get it settled."

Ray Evans was the county sheriff, a stern man who'd done a good job modernizing the sheriff's office. He was also born and bred in Tall Pines. Finding a more impartial judge—someone who wanted what was best for the town—was probably impossible. Even if she had a hunch he might be a fisherman.

Maybe he'd hate the suggestion of having more competition. She'd be sure to hit on that point.

"Fine." Dean shrugged like a man who had few cares. Elaine raised her chin and nodded, determined to appear just as confident.

"Sounds good. Is it… Ah, it's still okay for my mother to stay, right? Just tonight?" She hated the uncertainty in her voice.

"Sure thing. I got the first room ready while you were working in town this morning." Dean smiled. "Just in case."

Suspicious, Elaine turned to her mother and found her studying the garden. Maybe she hadn't shown up at just the right moment. Maybe she'd had help getting there in the nick of time.

And her arrival had made Elaine so happy she wasn't sure how annoyed she should be.

"We'll head on upstairs, then." Elaine opened the screen door but paused as Dean said, "Oh, and I bought the groceries we need for a nice dinner. Roast's already in the slow cooker, Mrs. Stillman."

"Excellent news, Dean. I'll get started on the rest." She hurried past Dean, avoided Elaine's suspicious frown and swept up the stairs. "There's that beautiful wallpaper. I'll never forget the first time I saw it. I told your father we had to have it."

A few important questions trembling on the tip of her tongue, Elaine followed her up the stairs. "What did he say to that?"

"'A week of staring at it once a year's enough, Cath,'" her mother answered in a gruff voice.

Elaine wouldn't have responded well to that kind of comment, either.

When they reached the first room, she could see that Dean had put out fresh linens before he opened the curtains to let in the afternoon sunshine. Maybe he had what it took to run the Bluebird, fishing camp or not.

Elaine set her mother's bag on the bed. "Want to tell me what sort of cozy arrangement you and Dean have cooked up?"

Her mother slowly turned away from the window. She licked her lips and did a leisurely tour of the room, running her hand lightly over the furniture. "He texted me Wednesday, said his father should be arriving today or tomorrow so the decision would be coming quickly. If I wanted to stay, I was welcome, and he really thought this was the time." She clasped her hands in front of her. "I told my boss I needed a few days, texted Dean with a short grocery list—because I have every intention of wowing you with my newest skills—and packed up the car."

Elaine eased down on the bed. Her mother sat next to her and wrapped one arm around her shoulders. "I'd have come Wednesday if I'd known you needed me,

Lainey. I'm sorry. You're so strong. I guess I don't think of you needing my help the way I need yours."

Elaine sighed. "That's more my fault than yours, Mom. I'm starting to see that now."

Just like she was coming to understand that having it all together could be the symptom of something really wrong. Or at least the insane insistence that everyone else think she had it all together.

Because she didn't.

"And to be honest, I didn't want to come." Her mother sighed. "I'm ashamed. I didn't want to confront the memories."

"I have such trouble understanding that," Elaine said. "I loved it here. We were so happy." She made nervous pleats in her scrubs. "Weren't we?"

"We were good at pretending, especially a week at a time." Her mother stood up to look in the closet and came back to pull a stack of clothing out of her suitcase. "It's hard to fight when the neighbors are so close. You remember this place differently than I do. All I really remember is biting back way too much honesty. Your father never really had that problem."

Elaine covered her face with both hands and tried to catch her breath. She'd been wrong all along. "Wow."

Her mother sat next to her. "But on the way up here I decided none of that matters. It's in the past. You are going to make this inn fabulous, and I can look forward to some great times here. When you win, I'm going to do everything I can to help."

Elaine took a deep breath. "I needed to hear that. Whether we do it here or somewhere else, we're going to make good memories." When she'd started this, she'd had some noble notion of giving her mother a purpose, pulling her out of her rut and giving them both something to bond over.

Now her mother had a new job, a new hobby and a new friend. And Elaine had learned that her wonderful memories were heavy on fiction. She'd been obsessed with the promise of an exciting future...

Well, that future was as possible anywhere else as it was here. The Bluebird wasn't magic.

If she wanted the exciting future, she'd

have to create it, no matter how this bet was decided.

Overwhelmed again, Elaine flopped on the bed to stare up at the ceiling.

"Seems that handsome young man is more than someone who wants to win a competition." Her mother waited patiently for Elaine to figure out how to answer the question that wasn't really a question.

"We've gotten to know each other while we worked." Elaine ignored her mother's stare. The kiss should not come up. If it did, her mother wouldn't be content until Elaine and Dean were exchanging vows. No matter how often Elaine ignored her dating advice, her mother never gave up hope.

Catherine Stillman, true-blue romantic. This was one more place where she and her mother were so different it was hard to believe they were related.

Her mom sighed. "Well, I guess that's a start." Then she tapped her lips with a finger. "Now tell me about his father. He seems…nice." Before Elaine could launch into a lecture about focusing on what was important and forgetting men for a while, her mother winked and squeezed her shoulder. "I'm kidding. Sort of."

Elaine laughed, willing to lighten the mood again. Maybe all she'd ever needed to do was involve her mother in her life more, not less.

She needed her mom sometimes. That was perfectly all right. Normal, even. Her mother loved it. Why did Elaine have such a problem showing it?

And how had this man, who'd known her for less than a full month, seen through Elaine's pretending that she had everything under control? How did he manage to do the one thing that would make whatever happened okay?

CHAPTER FOURTEEN

DEAN FLIPPED SLOWLY through the slideshow of shots his father had taken on the road. "So, the Grand Canyon, Hoover Dam and the Pacific Ocean. Not a bad haul for a little over three weeks." He stopped on a shot of a donkey. "Please tell me you didn't ride this donkey."

"Mule. That's a mule. And I did. It was that or a helicopter ride, and you know how I am about heights." His dad waved his hands. "Given the choice, I'll pick sticking to the ground whenever I can."

Just like Elaine.

At least he didn't say it out loud.

"Some people don't do either, Dad. Some people are content to just…look. You know, go to the observation areas and observe." He couldn't get over some of the shots his dad had gotten. Clearly this trip had been about more than observing.

There was a lot of action and adventure in these photos.

"Might never get back to the Grand Canyon. Had to see everything I could. A couple of times I wished that chance hadn't come along, mainly while I was looking over the edge, but you can't beat the view from the bottom. Once in a lifetime." He wagged his finger. "I mean that. I'm not ever doing it again."

Dean laughed and clapped his father on the back. "These are some great shots to remember the trip. Was it what you thought it would be?"

"Hard to say." His dad ran a hand down the back of his neck. "Saw some landmarks I always dreamed of. Took a surfing lesson just because."

Trying to picture his dad on a surfboard took real concentration. Luckily, there was a picture of that, too. "This isn't a late midlife crisis, is it?" The grin on his father's face as he carried a surfboard across the sand was contagious.

"Maybe it's the old man getting a touch of the restless, adventurous spirit that makes you climb mountains and race into danger." His dad shrugged. "Gotta say, after riding that mule and living to tell the tale, I think I understand what drives you. Hope it's not permanent, though. Only so much adrenaline this old heart can take."

"Looks like it did you some good," Dean said. "You haven't stopped smiling since you got home."

"Oh, this trip was what I needed. Gave me a whole new outlook. But if you think these smiles come from a vacation, you're mistaken." His dad shut the laptop. "I can't get over how good this place looks. You look better, too, less like a man clinging to a ledge. The doctor had something to do with that, I bet."

Dean narrowed his eyes. "Right. Want to tell me what kind of favor she was doing for you?"

"You caught that, huh?" His father ran a hand over his mouth. "Just asked her to see if she could find out what was bothering you. I remember how staring out a dark window all night long can wear on a man."

Dean crossed his arms over his chest and considered that. He'd spent hours thinking about all the things he should have shared with his father. Here was a chance. "I have nightmares. I dream about gunfights or near misses or the last explosion. Sometimes I can't fall asleep. Other times I wake up with my heart racing and my whole body sweating and shivering. Sometimes I lie awake regretting my decisions, like the ones that made you think you were better off handling this place and your health and whatever else you've managed to make it through all alone. And sometimes I'm angry, and I don't really know why." He closed his eyes.

"But you should know, when the world exploded and I was sure I was going to die, all I wanted was to talk to you one more time. I wouldn't have had the right words then just like I don't—"

Whatever was about to spill out of his mouth was muffled against his father's shoulder as his dad wrapped his arms around him.

"When she died, I couldn't stay here," Dean said. "Everywhere I turned, there was something that made it hurt again."

"And I couldn't stand the thought of ever letting her go." His father's voice was quiet.

"But I learned something on this trip. She's not tied to this place. She goes with me."

His father stepped back. "That first sight of the ocean reminded me of the postcards she used to collect. She would have loved that part of the trip." He smoothed a hand over his forehead. "She certainly would've been a much better surfer. Couldn't be worse than me."

Dean rubbed the ache in his chest that used to come every single time he thought of his mother. Over the years, he'd gotten more vigilant, stopping the memories before they formed. Now he was sorry it had taken him so long to realize how much comfort there was in remembering.

"So many nights I've clutched my phone in my hand, ready to call you for help—" Dean stopped to clear his throat "—and I pictured home. Thank you for holding on to it for me."

His dad cleared his throat and blinked hard before he said, "You use that phone next time. You make the call. No matter where you are, here or in Timbuktu. You call."

Dean nodded. They shook hands and

just like that, everything was better. The air was clear. No matter how this turned out, he and his dad were okay.

"Ready to do this?" His dad waved a hand vaguely. "Ready to take the Bluebird, change it up, make it yours?"

"You bet." He was. Really. Any doubts he might have could be handled with hard work and pushing ahead. The past few weeks had shown him that. "I didn't know what I was looking for when I came home, but I feel better, more myself here. Painting felt like therapy."

"And what about the doctor? Ready to see the last of her for a while?"

Dean's father was studying his face intently. Dean stifled the urge to shake his head.

"I imagine she's not an easy person to bump along with," his dad said. "Too driven. Got no take-it-easy in her." His father smiled innocently. Tossing out his bait, waiting for Dean to jump on it.

"We both had to learn about relaxation. She works harder than anybody I've ever met, and she's good at everything." Except knitting but on the second lesson, she'd whip out a sweater with one hand while she made a scarf with the other. "Is this your version of matchmaking?"

He never would've expected it from his dad, the guy who'd holed up like some fishing hermit after his mother died.

A love like that, one that had lasted all these years apart, might make Robert Collins the biggest romantic Dean knew.

A guy like that could have some solid advice on romance.

"If it was, I'd say I'm talented at it. Took one shot, scored a direct hit. That's what we call accuracy in the business." His father made finger guns and blew away imaginary smoke. "I also learned something about myself in the process. This is home and I love it, but there's an awful lot out there in the world. I've got to go after it."

At a loss for words, Dean nodded. He couldn't argue with that. Finally he said, "I hope this turns out the way you intended, Dad. I understand this crazy urge to see the world. I don't get wagering the future of the Bluebird in a competition with someone like Elaine Watson. I could lose this. It wouldn't even be a shock."

And it scared him, so he hadn't spent much time considering "what if." He didn't want to disappoint his father. He didn't want to lose this fragile new connection to the memories of his mother. Now that he knew how much he wanted to win, he was afraid of losing.

"Have faith, son." His dad squeezed his shoulder.

Of course. His father wouldn't let the Bluebird go to Elaine if he was convinced that Dean would stay. He could change the game if that's the way it turned out.

"I trust you, Dad."

Then he remembered that Elaine Watson would not take losing easily and wondered how much it would hurt to lose her friendship.

"Good, but I meant have faith in yourself. Even if you lose, you've got your whole life ahead of you. Nothing but possibility. We could hit the road together. You could build your own spot somewhere quiet and do exactly what you want instead of dealing with chores and boarders. You could even get your old job back."

His father wouldn't come right out and ask the big question: What would Dean do if he lost? After all this time, he had no answer.

"And as far as faith goes, try having faith in her, too." His father checked his watch. "It's about time. Got all your stuff? Let's head downstairs."

Dean took a deep breath and patted his laptop. "Sure thing. It's all right here."

At the bottom of the staircase, he could hear conversation coming from outside. He glanced at his father. "Sounds like the judges are here."

Edna and Jackie were sitting in the rocking chairs, staring hard in opposite directions. The battle lines were clearly drawn. Ray Evans was ambling through the neatly manicured yard while Elaine's mother pointed out Elaine's improvements to the garden.

Mark Taylor had his camera out and was taking shots of the lake, the revitalized porch, the judges and the bluebird boxes.

"Where's Elaine?" Dean asked. He nodded at Mark and Jackie and then bent to kiss Edna's cheek. When she jerked away and shoved her hand in his direction, he shook it and nodded at her narrow-eyed stare.

"Inside. Setting the stage." Jackie wagged his eyebrows, and Dean had a bad feeling his presentation skills were about to be seriously overshadowed.

His suspicion was confirmed when Elaine stepped out onto the porch in her sundress, the one she'd been wearing when they were introduced.

"If you're prepared, we can get started."

The small group followed her into the front sitting room, the home of the fussy antiques. The last time he'd been in this room, all the furniture was covered, but now the old sheets were gone and the wood gleamed, as if his mother were about to step through the swinging door from the kitchen.

And Elaine Watson had her game face on. She had posters, her own laptop and a fancy binder on display in front of a table where Edna, Jackie and Ray Evans sat. Delicate cups and saucers were arranged in a circle around his mother's pink tea service.

She'd come to win.

A flood of adrenaline and old-fashioned will to win pumped through him. Dean grinned. She was going to make this a battle.

He liked her even more for it.

His father raised his eyebrows before settling into a chair. Elaine passed out the delicate pink cups along with vibrant pictures of the newly painted Bluebird, including a photo that Elaine had no doubt taken with the camera she'd asked to borrow.

Her mother poured hot tea into the cups, looking every bit the perfect hostess. She'd be able to greet guests and make them feel comfortable, a trait he wasn't sure he had.

Then she put a truly amazing pastry in front of his father. Apple filling spilled out the side, and he suddenly wanted that pastry more than he'd ever wanted any other pastry in the world.

"Surely that's cheating." Somehow. It had to be.

He'd brought spreadsheets to a pastry fight.

ELAINE TOOK A deep breath and motioned to the seat at the end of the table. "Mark, would you like to sit?"

"Nah, I'll stand. Get some action shots for the story. If that's all right?"

Elaine clasped her hands in front of her. "Fine. If Dean has no objection, I'll go first. Then after we both present, we can take questions before you decide." She glanced at Dean to see him perch on the edge of a chair and wave at Edna, who gave him a wink.

Elaine realized she'd been staring when her mother motioned with her head in the direction of all Elaine's hard work. "Right. In front of you are the highlights of my plan. As you can see, renovation efforts have already begun with fresh paint on the outside. I've cleared the garden in preparation for some nice fall planting. The road is in good working order." Thanks to Dean… "As soon as I'm given the go-ahead and the purchase is completed, Nick Robertson and I will address the interior renovation. The first priority is a modernized kitchen."

Her mother murmured, "Oh, yes it is." She pulled out a poster that showed the paint colors and cabinets Elaine had chosen. The revised layout would allow plenty of room for high-end appliances and a long bar for seating.

"The new Bluebird will focus on a full family experience. I'll offer fun classes for kids and families. Cooking, knitting, photography…" She glanced at Dean and then looked away. "Guests will be taught by local professionals. We might even have some fishing guides come in to work with the kids. This would be a real bonus for some families." Because not everyone was lucky enough to have a father to teach them how to bait a hook or find their way out of the woods. The Bluebird could be a real benefit to single parents, something she'd just realized as she was talking.

"I believe we could open the inn in three months. And of course, the tearoom will reopen as soon as possible after that. My mother has agreed to take the day-to-day oversight of the hotel because I intend to keep my practice." Elaine motioned at the amazing pastries in front of them and desperately hoped her mother had held a few back. If she didn't get one, she might be more disappointed than if she lost the Bluebird. "And she'll bake."

She folded her hands together and waited for them to try the apple dumpling. "Mom, Dean doesn't have one. Would you…" She watched her mother slide a plate in front of him and nearly smiled at his suspicious look.

She wanted him to comprehend how hard this victory was going to be.

Everyone took a bite. No one said a thing until Jackie jumped up and said, "I'll pay you twice what she's paying to supply the Country Kitchen." He frowned at Elaine as if he was seeing her in a brand-new light. "Mona's pies got nothing on these." Then he said, pointing around the room, "And if any of you tell her I said that, I'll sue." Jackie sat and finished his pastry with another glare in her direction.

Somehow she'd managed to lose her own judge.

Her mother stood behind the judges and urged her to continue.

"Finally, here are some shots of the Bluebird where I've tried to capture what it means to me. Most of you know that my family visited Tall Pines when I was a girl. I remember these rocking chairs and that view and so many afternoons when Martha Collins would include me and my mom in whatever she was doing around the house." She waved her arms, happy with the memory of the freedom she'd had here. "This was a place where I could be anything. I could be a scientist in the morning, a grand lady in the afternoon and a screaming kid flying from a rope swing after dinner. That's what I want to rebuild. If you give me this chance, the Bluebird Bed-and-Breakfast can be that kind of place again, one where families get stronger and kids have a chance to explore."

Dean's expression was hard to read. Robert Collins was smiling, and Ray Evans was studying the figures in the packet. Edna had her arms crossed over her chest and a teacup in one hand.

Jackie was craning his neck to see if there were any more pastries.

Without another word, Elaine sat.

"My turn?" Dean asked as he pulled his laptop out. Not sure she wanted to stay for this, she nodded.

No, Elaine. You stay. Listen. Whatever points he makes, you come up with reasonable alternatives. That's how you win this. You can't quit now.

"Well, my presentation is a little less… polished, but you'll see I've done some careful research on things Tall Pines and Spring Lake might need." He started his slideshow. A photo of the view in front of the Bluebird came up, with a computer-generated drawing of a boxy building standing roughly where the dock was now.

Elaine was no designer, but if she was going to ruin the view, she'd demand something better than a big wooden box.

"First thing we'll do is build a small marina, right here in front of the inn. Fishermen want a handy space to store the boat, and we can sell gas and bait."

Dean walked toward Elaine and paused in front of her while he made his next point. "You may have heard a rumor that I was planning a restaurant. A better alternative would be a small grill or snack shop run right out of the marina, a place where boats can stop for a quick bite. The only other store like that is in Lawrence.

A snack shop would expand the Bluebird's reach, require more employees and bring in more taxes."

Edna's lips moved along with every word Dean spoke. They'd rehearsed this presentation well. He clicked the slideshow and a hand-drawn map of the cove came up. "Once the marina is completed and the docks are repaired, I'll begin to offer day tours and fishing packages while a small line of cabins is built along the shoreline here." He pointed to the trail he and Elaine had jogged along. The view from those cabins would be amazing. "We'll outfit them with kitchenettes, but everyone will need to come to town for full meals." Elaine watched Jackie nod in satisfaction.

"As far as the inn goes, we're going to modernize with a view to comfortable function."

Comfortable function…did that mean something other than new furniture?

He pulled up a spreadsheet. "I don't expect you can read this, but I've outlined a budget for renovation and new builds, possible five-year income and a timeline for each phase." His voice faded as Ray Evans picked up the laptop and hauled it closer. Robert Collins looked over his shoulder and Dean slumped in his chair.

"Have we reached the question-and-answer part yet, Miss Bossy?" Edna asked with a sniff.

Wishing she could say no, Elaine bared her teeth in a smile. "Go ahead."

"What about families?" Edna sipped her tea and looked serenely at Dean. "Where do they fit in your plan?"

Dean seemed as shocked as Elaine felt. Edna was his judge. She should be attacking Elaine, right?

He shrugged awkwardly. "Well, they would be drawn to the marina. Of course." Then he frowned. "And I guess kids and spouses would be welcome. But my proposal was to create a camp for…serious fishermen."

Ray and Jackie sent uncomfortable peeks toward Edna.

They both had had wives.

And they probably had an idea how well a serious fishing retreat would go over.

"If you'll recall, I did mention that many men enjoy spending vacations with their families, teaching their children about the things they love," Edna said. She scanned down the table, and Robert and Ray nodded. "We talked about making the inn family friendly. What happened to that, Dean?" She said the last while gritting her teeth, and Elaine felt a surge of hope that Dean might have managed to lose his own judge as easily as she'd flipped Jackie to the other side with a beautiful dessert.

"I thought about it. I decided against it." The flush on his cheeks matched the hesitation in his words. "I want a place that fits my style. This adventure focus is me."

"And what about women who love to fish or hike or climb mountains? Are they welcome?" Edna smiled. "I don't know any but I imagine they exist."

"Of course they're welcome." Dean tugged on the neck of his T-shirt. "Just, they'll have to…you know…"

"Leave their hair dryers at home?" Edna dared him to agree.

Dean wisely kept his mouth shut.

"And you. Didn't I tell you not to forget the dads?" Edna asked with a sniff. People who rejected her advice were going to get no mercy.

"I didn't. I have a list of fishing guides, two of whom I've already talked to about running special tours through the fall. We can advertise together, and I'll make sure anyone who wants to fish finds a guide."

Edna pursed her lips.

"This grill. Lunch only?" Jackie asked.

"That's where we'll start. Lunch only. Summer only. But if demand is big enough, we'll expand the hours." Dean looked sorry to add the last part, and she admired him for telling the truth.

"What do you think, Ray?" Robert asked, a concerned frown on his face.

The sheriff stretched in his chair and pondered the question for a long second. Then he looked at Elaine and Dean. "Well, now… Both plans have merit."

Everyone at the table swapped glances as if they were making sure everyone else expected more, too.

Ray sighed. "Gotta say, though, if we're looking at what's best for the town, it's going to be families, not a bunch of wild men looking to cut up on the weekend.

Families will support the shops in town, the restaurants will do a bigger business and the crowd will be completely different, meaning fewer late-night calls when some idiot drinks too many beers and decides to give night fishing a try." He tapped his finger on his knee and frowned. "I'm only saying that because of conversations I've had with Murphy in Lawrence. He gets a call every weekend for some thing or another happening at the Spring Lake Oasis."

The surprise on the faces around the table suggested no one had considered the differences in the kind of tourists the new inn would bring. Just like that, Elaine felt a glimmer of hope.

"Of course, this new marina would be a boost to our side of Spring Lake. We could draw in a fishing tournament, maybe, or even sponsor one. The thing about fishermen is that if they find a spot they love, they come back. If the fish are biting, they'll plan more than one vacation a year. We could be looking at a much bigger percentage of return visits." Ray pointed at the laptop screen. "Which Dean has taken into account. That could mean big things for Tall Pines."

He picked up his teacup and sipped calmly as though he hadn't thrown a big question mark over the conversation.

"Well, now…" Robert rubbed his forehead. "We've got some talking to do. Maybe you could wait outside?"

Dean nodded. "Sure." He motioned for Elaine to walk in front of him, and Mark followed them out.

"Are you up for a picture together?" Mark asked and trotted down the front steps.

Elaine glanced at Dean and saw him shrug. "Sure. Where do you want us?"

Mark looked up and down the porch. "How about this corner? I can get the fresh paint and the bluebird boxes in the background."

Elaine followed Dean and stood stiffly next to him, thinking they probably looked like an updated version of Grant Wood's American Gothic.

"Too bad I left my pitchfork in the garage," Dean muttered.

Elaine smiled as Mark snapped the shot.

"Good. Now I'll head to the dock. Grab

some landscape photos." She and Dean watched him trot down the hill.

"So what should we pretend to talk about?" Dean asked. He motioned to her usual rocking chair before dropping down into the one beside it.

"You did a good job," she said grudgingly as she eased down to sit beside him. Dean laughed.

"Why do you sound so surprised? I'm a professional photographer, and I've worked with some of the finest news agencies in the world. Did you think I was nothing more than a pretty face?"

Elaine smiled and took a moment to study Dean. Sleeping through the night had softened the harsh lines around his eyes.

And she was in serious trouble.

"How does it feel to lose to a girl?" She crossed her arms tightly over her chest.

"You know, life goes on. If you win, I'll…" He stared at the lake. "Well, I'll figure out what comes next."

"Sure. There's no need to worry about me, either." She crossed one leg over the other and kicked one foot in a quick pattern. "There's plenty of work to keep me busy in Tall Pines."

Pride was a dangerous thing, but she didn't want pity from Dean. He thought she was strong. That's the way she wanted everyone to see her.

He also knew about her hidden wounds and had enough of his own to be compassionate. And funny and strong and smart, but those qualities really had nothing to do with the situation and everything to do with the man.

Right now, they were both in the same spot: they had everything to lose and no control over the outcome. Even if she lost, Elaine wanted to remember finally understanding someone else this well.

DEAN WATCHED MARK walk along the shoreline and wondered if putting up a marina was worth losing the serenity of this view. He'd been so certain before because it was the least expensive spot and the fastest way to get the biggest return on his money, but it might be the point that lost him the whole thing.

To distract himself, he watched Elaine's

bouncing foot, the only real sign of her nerves.

"I'm not sure how to thank you for bringing my mother. You were scared for a second when the apple dumplings came out. Admit it." The satisfaction in her voice was cute, even if she was right.

"Just like you didn't expect your judge to flip to my side after one bite. Admit it."

She straightened the folds of her sundress. "Possible miscalculation."

"Well, if you lose, you can blame that." Dean shook his head. It had been a smart move. The problem was that people were unpredictable.

"All right. We're ready." His dad held the door open.

Elaine's mother was packing up all the remaining pastries. Jackie, Edna and Ray were gathered around the table. Once Elaine and Dean had stepped into the room, everyone turned to look at them.

"All right, tell us," Elaine said from her spot in the doorway. Her hands were clenched into tight fists and her chin raised. She was preparing for the worst. He wanted to rest his hands on her shoulders, ease them back down and tell her it would all be fine. No matter what, she'd be fine.

He also understood her well enough to know she wouldn't appreciate anything that looked like pity.

"Both of you have impressive plans," Robert said. "And I can tell from all the improvements you've already made that Martha's inn will be in capable hands no matter who I choose. The problem is, neither one of you is going to accept anything less than a clear win so…" Robert scratched his chin. "The judges have decided Elaine's plan is best. I raised a family here. The Bluebird should be about family."

The worry was clear on his father's face, but if he said anything else, Dean couldn't hear it over the static in his ears. When Elaine rested her hand on his chest and leaned forward, he could hear, "Are you okay? Here. Sit down."

Her concern rattled him, brought him back to reality. He cleared his throat. "Uh, yeah. Caught off guard is all." He forced a smile and surveyed the room without meeting anyone's eyes. "Guess I should have spent some time packing." Not that it would take long to shove all his clothes in the backpack.

"There's no rush," Elaine said. "We'll be renovating and there's so much space. Just...stay. Please."

"We're about to hit the road. Father-son excursion. We'll go see how the West was won." Despite his father's cheerful answer, everyone in the room studied Dean closely, sympathy easy to read in their expressions.

The way the judges watched him, small frowns of concern on their faces and their hands stretched out as though they were half a second away from patting him on the shoulder, reminded him of the days right after his mother's funeral. His father had done the same thing then, too, pretended everything was going to be fine when the whole world was changing.

Losing his mother had been a blow.

He'd honestly never thought he could lose.

And he had to get out.

"First, I think I'll..." His shoulders slumped. He couldn't even come up with anywhere to escape to. This had been his retreat.

When it looked as if his father was about to try to comfort him, Dean turned and went up the stairs, taking them two at a time. In the bedroom he'd desperately planned to escape—until he'd needed it just as desperately to recover—he jammed all his ragged clothes into his backpack and carefully packed his cameras and equipment. Then he sat on the bed and braced his hands on his knees.

He could stay. Elaine's offer had been sincere. There was no need to rush off.

Except staying here would hurt. Every person he met would console him or try to cheer him up with hollow words, but they'd only be reminding him of what a huge loss this was. Delaying the inevitable made no sense.

He had to go.

Quickly. With as little fuss as possible.

When he was sure he could pull off a convincing "no worries" expression, he slung his backpack over his shoulder and picked up his equipment bag. Then he carefully navigated the stairs, unsurprised to see everyone hovering at the bottom.

"Please, Dean, just stay tonight. There's so much time to figure out what comes next." Elaine held out a hand. "We still have to meet with the lawyer and the bank. Then there's renovation. In the meantime, you can… I'll even climb the mountain with you in the morning. The crazy way and everything!"

She should be gloating. That was what winners did. Maybe that would have been enough to cause him to dig in, stay out of orneriness. Just as she'd done in the beginning because she wanted the Bluebird so badly.

But now she wore the same worried expression his father did. Instead of being matter-of-fact about his loss, like she had during his confessions about the nightmares and insomnia, she was hurting for him.

He hated that. It looked like pity.

"I can't stay." He took her hand and drew her close for a goodbye kiss. Conscious of their audience, he pulled away before he was ready and the way she blinked slowly up at him eased the pinch of losing. "I have to…make some plans."

Edna patted his shoulder. "Good idea. Leave 'em wanting more. We'll go look at rental property." She rummaged in her tracksuit pocket. "Got the apartment for you." She held out a card. They both ignored the way his hand trembled when he took it.

A place of his own in Tall Pines? Was that what he really wanted next? What would he do? What would keep the nightmares away now?

Maybe he should just get back to the job, pick up his camera and chase the old memories away with new ones. His stay at Spring Lake had been a nice vacation. Was it time to go to work, dodge some bullets, tell an important story? At least he'd be doing something with his life.

He wasn't sure what he said as he left but he was halfway across the yard when his dad shouted, "Dean, wait!" Half of him wanted to storm off. He'd trusted his father to make sure he won. Instead, he was lost again.

But he hadn't quite forgotten all the

lessons he'd learned while rebuilding the Bluebird, so he turned slowly.

"You forgot this." His father held out his laptop and then pulled him close for a hug. "Wherever you want to go, we'll go. Together."

When he stepped back Dean could see the promise in his father's eyes, but that was the problem. He didn't want to go anywhere.

And he sure didn't want to hold his father back now that he'd discovered living again.

"Just consider it." His father slugged his arm in another attempt to make sure they both knew everything was going to be fine. "Meet me at Jackie's for breakfast. I'll bring a map."

Instead of arguing, Dean nodded. Before he could get the door closed, Edna was hustling across the lawn. "Wait for me. I need a ride to town. Jackie drives like a maniac. Don't know how he keeps a license."

Unable to fight the fatigue that settled over his shoulders or the firm stare of the small woman waiting impatiently next to his Jeep, Dean held Edna's door open and waited for her to slide in. When he was settled behind the wheel, he took one last look at the Bluebird with the fresh paint and the dock he was going to miss in the middle of the night.

And Elaine stood on the steps, framed beautifully by the bright blue shutters.

She wiped under her eyes and wrapped her arms around her waist. Tears were just about the only emotion he hadn't seen on her face. He hated seeing them now.

He made a jerky turn to drive away and took a deep breath. Nothing was forever. The Bluebird would be around a lot longer than either him or Elaine.

"All right, speed demon. Don't make me regret my charitable impulse." Edna had both hands braced on the dashboard. "Those red signs with the white letters mean stop, not speed up."

Dean tightened his grip on the steering wheel but lifted his foot off the accelerator.

"In a hurry, are you? One setback and you're headed out of town." Edna sniffed. "All those stories and you're just as scared as the rest of us."

He glanced over to see her slowly shaking her head. "Well, except the rest of us manage to stick around. We don't run when things get hard."

Dean clenched his jaw to hold back his angry answer. The jab landed hard in his abdomen, just as she intended. Then he muttered, "Where should I let you out?"

Edna grunted. "Take me to Shady Pines. Got some news to share. Time's wastin'."

The urge to zoom through town was hard to fight but he did. As he passed a small strip of apartments, Edna jingled a set of keys. "You might not remember this, but I own those apartments. Unit four is lightly furnished and has a lovely view of the alley behind the Smokehouse." She held a single key between her thumb and forefinger. "If you were to decide to try something new this time, to work through the disappointment and hurt, you could stay there. Rent free." She put a hand to her chest. "Believe me, that offer pains me. That's how you know I care."

He carefully took the key instead of snatching it out of her fingers. "You know, for someone who was supposed to be my judge, you're taking this defeat well."

"I've still got high hopes for you, Dean Collins, all current evidence to the contrary," Edna grumbled.

Desperate for another solution, he braced his arm against the steering wheel and said, "Hope that I'll do…what?" Maybe she had a clue to the third option, an alternative to going back to the only other life he'd lived.

"Something new." She patted his shoulder. "Dream bigger. Martha Collins raised a strong, brave man. Go ahead and prove it."

Before he could go open her door, Edna hopped out and slammed it shut. "You remember my new gallery, right?" She raised her eyebrows. "Seems like a man of your talents should investigate it. If you decide you'd like to be a part of our grand opening, you call me. You could be a big star here. I'm never wrong."

He had no time to answer because Edna was already hustling up the walk to Shady Pines, already enjoying the sweet taste of having fresh news no one could possibly have heard yet.

Dean turned the key over and over in his hand as he stared through the windshield. Then he put the Jeep in Drive and headed slowly out of town.

CHAPTER FIFTEEN

"WELL…" HER MOTHER tried to start a new conversation, took a long look at her face and lapsed into silence again.

Elaine didn't blame her. Dean had left even after she'd asked him, almost begged him, to stay. The brave expression she'd plastered on until the judges and Robert Collins had disappeared had melted into an ugly mess. She was still collapsed in her rocking chair in the cheerful sundress she'd put on as a sign of faith that she'd soon be hosting visitors from her front porch. That vision had been clear in her head the whole time she'd been working on her plan to restore the Bluebird.

The tense goodbye that had come after winning had never been a part of the plan.

Why was getting exactly what she dreamed of breaking her heart?

All the things she'd been working for could happen now. Her mother would come to stay. Her father could visit and bring his sons. They could even fish together. Get-togethers with the ladies from Purl's Place would give her a chance to show off a beautiful home and distract people from her terrible knitting. Tea on the front porch. Fall planting. Visits from her own bluebirds. She was on track for all those things.

But there would be no more Dean to challenge her or encourage her or make her feel safe and normal and real even when she messed up.

He'd totally ruined her plan.

And instead of being mad about that, all she wanted was for him to stay.

At least the tears had finally stopped. She'd been afraid that once they'd started, they'd go on forever.

How did her mother stand this pain let alone being out of control of her emotions again and again?

"Are there any more of those apple dumplings left?" she asked without turning her head. "Maybe you could shove one in my open mouth. Surely that will help."

Her mother laughed.

Elaine wasn't entirely sure she was joking.

She stared out across the lake and tried to ignore how her eyes burned and she needed to blow her nose. Her mother held a plate out in front of her. After treating herself to a sugar overload, Elaine told herself to get a grip.

"Winning that feels like losing. Have I completely lost my mind?"

Her mother sighed and sat beside her. "Nope. Love will do that to you." She patted Elaine's arm. "I have been there."

And she kept trying. "Are you crazy, Mom? Hurting like this is worse than I remembered." And she'd never do it again.

"As bad as it hurts when it ends, love is awesome when it works." The creaks of her mother's rocker reminded her of the connection she'd felt with Dean, sitting there in that same spot. And she was absolutely right. Letting go, trusting someone else for once, had been freeing.

She'd miss that connection until it came around again.

Elaine had to admire her mother's op-

timism in the face of so much heartbreak.
Never giving up was its own form of bravery.

All her life, she'd prided herself on doing
hard things without fear. But she'd just let
Dean walk away.

*You asked him to stay. That was brave,
Elaine.*

"Love. That wasn't supposed to happen.
We just met. We don't even have that much
in common." And if it was love, how could
he walk away?

Unless she was the only one experienc-
ing it.

"Forget about how it happened. Poets and
songwriters have been trying to figure out
what causes that spark for centuries. Worry
about what you're going to do about it."
Her mother's pragmatic tone was hard to
argue with.

But for the first time in a long while,
Elaine was stuck on what to do next. She'd
asked Dean to stay, but he'd left. What else
could she do?

"For now, I'm going to focus on my
plans. Tomorrow I'll introduce you to my
contractor. Then we're going to the bank

and the hardware store. I've got a promise to keep. I'm going to restore the Bluebird."

"CONGRATULATIONS," NICK SAID, clapping his hands together. "Robert gave me the go-ahead to begin demolition. Said you guys had hammered out the sale price, and all that was left was the paperwork. Ready for a new kitchen?"

"So ready," Elaine's mother said with a sigh as she considered the ragged cabinets.

Elaine ran a hand over the slanted counter and thought she might be sorry to see some of her hard work disappear.

But it would be worth it. New Bluebird. New memories.

Maybe Dean had been right all along.

"Want to sling a sledgehammer?" Nick offered her the handle. "Tearing things up is fun."

Dean might say something like that. And he'd enjoy every bit of this.

"No, I'll leave that up to the professionals." She turned to go. "I'm headed into town."

"Thank you for giving me this project, Dr. Watson. I love building new, but more than that, I enjoy making old things shine. This farmhouse is going to be amazing." Nick ran a hand over the banister as he followed her to the front door. "Everything's on order at King's. Just approve it and write a big check." His grin was contagious.

"You're not too sad about losing the marina?" While she'd been unable to sleep last night, she'd taken a page out of Dean's book and listened to the night sounds from the end of the dock. The longer she'd sat there, the easier it was to imagine a marina, the traffic and the increased amenities for fishermen and their families.

And it distracted her from wondering how Dean was making it through the night.

"Not gonna lie. I was pumped to build it. That's something I've never done, and I do like a challenge."

"Elaine does, too," her mother said with a heavy sigh. "Always has."

"Do you still have the plans?" Elaine asked as she turned to look through the door at the lake. Maybe the marina was the missing piece she'd been looking for. "And if you do, could you use them but maybe move the location?" She stepped onto the porch and waited for Nick and her mother to join her before she walked to the dock. She pointed at the neck of the cove. "Over there. So we still have plenty of scenery." And a peaceful dock for long nights.

"You want to move the marina?" Nick propped his hands on his hips and studied the cove's shoreline. "Shouldn't be that hard, but it would double your budget. The biggest increase will be in laying utilities out there. I'll need to get some quotes on that, but I could have you up and running by early fall and give you plenty of time to prepare for next spring."

The idea of doubling her budget made it hard to breathe. Buying and renovating the house would take every bit of her savings and the loan she'd already discussed with the bank. To get access to that much more money, she'd have to take another look at her plans, make forecasts and solid guesses on income, and go back to the bank.

But Dean's vision for the marina felt right. It was a bridge from the past to the future.

"Okay," Elaine said, "as soon as you can get me the cost, we'll move forward. While

I'm at the bank, I'll start a new loan application, too."

Her mother bit her lip. "Are you sure? A mortgage that size is a serious commitment. Do you really want to stay in Tall Pines for the next ten years? Or longer?"

Elaine studied her mother's face. Did her mom want her to leave Tall Pines? In the end, it didn't matter. This was home. She'd never let the Bluebird go.

"Absolutely." She held her hand out to Nick. "When can you start? We'll need to open soon if I've got a mortgage payment every month."

"I've got a small crew that could start on the inn this week, but there'll be permits and things to figure out on the marina. I'll see what I can do to get the ball rolling. Right now." The gleam in his eye said the marina would definitely open on time.

"We can paint," Elaine's mother said. "Maybe save some money."

Things were starting to work out better than Elaine had expected.

"Fine." Nick turned to survey the hall. "Sure you want to keep the wallpaper?

Won't take us long to remove it, put up a nice, modern white."

From the beginning, Elaine had hoped to restore everything at the Bluebird the way it used to be. She stared up at the morning glories and tried to picture the entry without the blue flowers. She couldn't.

And she remembered her promise to Dean that if the morning glories in the garden didn't return, she'd plant new vines. She knew now that she'd never be able to go back to the way things were. But she didn't want to forget the good times, either.

"Nope. The wallpaper stays." She sighed. "But we are going to have to make some updates. New furniture. Bigger television." She shook her head. "But I'm not mounting fish anywhere ever."

Nick frowned at the left turn the conversation had taken. "Sure. Makes sense."

With the new marina, Elaine would have to come up with ideas to attract fishermen for repeat visits. Dean had been right about that, among other things.

Elaine followed Nick out to his truck.

When the dust cloud settled behind him, she went to sit on the end of the dock.

Somehow the peace she'd hoped to find there had disappeared.

CHAPTER SIXTEEN

AFTER SHE FINISHED with her last patient of the day, Elaine headed for downtown Tall Pines. She had one goal: a gallon of paint to freshen up the room she'd chosen as her own. Instead of moving into the family quarters, she'd squeezed into a tiny closet-like space that had a nice view of the dock.

Her mother had left that morning so she'd be home to work her Saturday shift at Bake and Take. Robert Collins had rolled out of town on Monday after his breakfast with Dean.

Or so she'd heard through the grapevine.

No one seemed to pass along the most important piece of the story: whether or not Dean was with him. Edna would know. Of course she would. She knew everything. But Edna was entirely too smart. If Elaine asked and found out that instead of leaving with Robert, Dean had packed up his ratty cutoffs and hit the road, she wasn't sure she could keep it together. And Edna would understand why.

All week long she'd been on an emotional roller coaster and feeling more and more like her mother every day.

Still, she listened to all the conversations in her office, checked the after-hours emergency clinic rosters for any suspicious broken bones that might be caused by falling off a mountain and…waited. She wasn't sure for what. When she slowed down, she held her phone like a talisman and debated whether to call him.

That morning Nick had shown up bright and early to take the old kitchen down to the studs. The refrigerator had been moved to the garage, and that meant even cereal was a lot of work. Picking up a sandwich from the Smokehouse would take the last of her energy.

Without her mother to distract her or the sounds of men tearing down the house, the weekend would be long and lonely. A project could help.

King's Hardware was busier than Elaine had expected. As she waited for Mr. King to hand over her paint, she wished she hadn't agreed to give the new doctor at the after-hours clinic her shift. Fridays were crazy, the perfect distraction.

Her phone beeped to remind her that she had a voice mail. She scrolled through her missed calls to see Dean's number.

Determined to be brave, she punched the button to listen to the message. "Elaine, it's Dean. I just wanted to make sure you saw this week's paper and… Well, I hope you're doing well."

That was it. Elaine listened to the message again to be sure she hadn't missed the five minutes in the middle where he professed his love or explained why he had to leave town.

But neither was there. Just "I hope you're doing well."

She thought about throwing the phone. But she had an audience.

"That sure is a lovely color, Dr. Watson." Mr. King slid the paint can across the counter.

"Thanks, Mr. King," she answered as she gripped the handle. She was hoping the light gray paint would make her new room seem bigger and still give the space a personal touch. She'd lived in her apartment for years without picking up a paintbrush. She wasn't going to make the same mistake in her new home.

"Nick mentioned you'd put the marina on hold until next year." King hummed as he counted her change. "Probably smart, but I sure was looking forward to a marina close to home. I hate heading to Lawrence every time I take the boat out."

Elaine fiddled with the paint can. "Well, it's only a delay, not a cancellation. I want to do it right. The Bluebird and the Collinses deserve that, you know?"

When she'd looked at the cost of doing the renovations and building the marina the way she wanted, the only smart thing to do was get the inn open first, start making some money and then expand.

But she hated the delay. Some of Dean's excitement had rubbed off on her.

And Nick had been disappointed. Besides that, running a bed-and-breakfast, even with her mother's help, was going to take some adjustment.

"Yeah, Dean said the same thing when

he was in here this morning." King nodded. "It's just solid business, I guess."

She wanted to leap across the counter and ask all the questions that had been building up inside her during the past week. How was Dean? Did he seem tired? Was he sleeping? Where was he staying? Apparently somewhere in Tall Pines. The relief that swept over her made it easier to smile and wave before she stepped out onto the sidewalk.

Where she nearly walked right into Edna.

"Slow down there, young lady," Edna snapped. "Running out of patients so you're making your own?" She tugged the edge of her jacket, and Elaine was speechless.

Edna was wearing a lovely black suit. Right there in the middle of Tall Pines, Edna was dressed like a high-society dame out for an evening of charity fund-raising and theater. Even her hair was different, a beautiful soft gray that made her look rich instead of eccentric.

"Well, are you going to apologize?" Edna's concerned frown reminded Elaine that she'd been gaping for entirely too long.

"Sorry." Elaine cleared her throat. "I apologize, Edna. I didn't see you there."

"Obviously. You were moving at full steam. Emergency somewhere?"

Elaine shifted the paint can. "Uh, no, just deep in thought."

Edna sniffed. "Oh, really. Wouldn't be about a certain photographer I know, would it?"

Feeling the pinch of the paint can handle, Elaine switched hands and tried to figure out how to answer that. "Well, maybe I was thinking about why I hadn't heard anything from him." All week long. Until today. And how disappointing that was.

"I guess he missed your call?" Edna tilted her head to the side.

Elaine fought the urge to squirm. "Well, no, but I've been busy." And mad. A little hurt. And jumping at the sound of every truck coming down the road. Each one belonged to one of Nick's crews. After deciding to postpone the marina, they'd finalized all the plans for the inn itself, and when she and Robert finished the closing, the Bluebird was going to become one solid construction area.

"Right, busier than finding a new place to live and figuring out what to do with the rest of your life, I guess." Edna shrugged. "And getting ready for an art show. He really has been slacking lately. You are coming tonight, aren't you?"

"I guess my invitation was lost in the mail," Elaine said with a frown. Had it been? Was he that…mad about losing? Surely not.

"There was no invitation," Edna muttered. "Mark put it in the paper. Tonight. Seven. Featuring stories from photojournalist Dean Collins and light hors d'oeuvres. Don't you read?"

This was the week of Mark's feature on the bet and the judges' decision. All she'd done was stare at the picture of them on the front page and fold it back up.

Edna rolled her eyes. "Good grief. Of course you missed it. Of course he didn't call you to make a point of inviting you. Because you both want to be miserable as long as possible and 'plan your future.'" The air quotes made Elaine snap to attention. "I swear you young people need to realize the future is happening right now, and you're missing the best part." Edna caught her wrist. "Never mind. Come with me."

"In these?" Elaine motioned at her wrinkled scrubs. "No way."

"That's a disappointment. To me and to Dean, I'd imagine. There are some shots on display that you need to see." Edna smiled and a shiver rolled over Elaine. When Edna knew something she didn't, Elaine had good cause to be concerned.

"Maybe if I hurry…" Elaine took a step back. Edna squeezed her hand once but let her go. Since almost everything she owned was still in her apartment, it would be a quick trip to change out of the scrubs.

If she wanted to go.

Edna made shooing motions. "Don't stand there. Hurry."

Before Elaine seized her chance to slide into her car, Edna said, "Elaine, you did an amazing job with your plans. Don't be stupid now."

Elaine froze. "What do you mean?"

"We've known each other a long time. I've been expecting you to move out of that tiny apartment for years. It's barely fit for a college kid, much less the town's beloved doctor." Edna wagged her finger. "Decide what you want and go after it. Don't waste any more days waiting for things to be what you want. Make them what you want. Just like you did with the Bluebird."

Elaine blinked, not sure she was awake. This had to be a dream, didn't it?

"Edna, why have you been so kind to me for so long? You rented that apartment to me at a steal, even for Tall Pines. You and I both know you could have evicted me and raised the rent several times." She'd often wondered how long Edna's charity would last, but she'd been afraid to ask the question until now.

"I don't change for change's sake, Dr. Watson, but I have to tell you I don't miss any opportunity, either. If the right renter had come along, you'd have been packed and on your way. That's smart business. So is offering a home to a young doctor who can make a difference in your community. My sister, over at Shady Pines, she needed a talented doctor who would consider new Alzheimer's treatments. You did that. I have a niece who's practically eleven months pregnant. That's the first in a long line, I hope. This town needs skilled doctors. I could see it when you came to town. There's something about you that convinces a person you can be trusted. I wanted the best for Tall Pines. I could sacrifice a little money to make that happen."

Elaine blinked, overcome with emotion, something that had never happened in a conversation with Edna and probably never would again.

"Don't disappoint me now, Elaine. Be as smart now as I knew you were then." Edna pointed at her and then marched down the sidewalk. "If you chicken out, like I can see perking there in your brain, I'll see you at Purl's in the morning. I'll be disappointed, but we can still knit together." Elaine watched her walk away until she realized she was baking in the sun and getting later every second.

On her way through town, she tried to picture the clothes hanging in her closet. "What do you wear to an art show in Tall Pines?" Elaine waved at Hailey and her mother as they crossed the street in front of the ice cream parlor. "Since it's the first one, maybe the dress code's kind of loose."

After she parked, she hurried inside to her closet. "Okay, so this black dress…" She swiped a few more hangers. "Or that black dress." Both had been worn to her mother's engagement parties. Both seemed to go along with Edna's night-at-the-theater duds. She yanked the second dress out and muttered a curse as she looked at the clock. There was no time to attempt eye liner, a feat that took her twice as long as other women, or to smooth the end-of-day mess from her hair. "Let Edna win best dressed. Just don't miss what's important."

Maybe by the time she made it to the gallery, she'd figure out what to say.

DEAN STARED INTO the bubbles of his ginger ale and wished for a nice dark corner to disappear into.

No such luck.

Tall Pines's new gallery was one wide-open cube with a wall of windows and enough people inside to eliminate all hope of escape. Plus, Edna was stuck to his side, a persistent, slightly annoying shadow. He couldn't quite get over the transformation from tracksuit to evening wear. She obviously felt the same.

"You look like a very, very expensive and yet sad accountant." Edna shoved a plate of cheese and crackers in his hand. "Eat something. That will help."

"You don't like my suit?" Dean popped a cheese cube into his mouth and chewed while he considered her description. He'd bought a new suit for the occasion and gotten his hair cut. Maybe he'd gone too far. "You wanted me to show up looking like Indiana Jones, didn't you?"

"Would have given the whole evening more wow factor. Guess your stories will have to bring the wow," Edna grumbled.

He nodded while he scanned the mingling crowd. The turnout was impressive. He hadn't expected a big showing in a small place like Tall Pines, but Edna must have traded in every bit of unused scuttlebutt she had to fill the room.

Whatever the reason, Tall Pines had showed up and dressed for the occasion.

He hoped he could go through with it. Disappointing a crowd this size would be hard.

And Edna would change the locks on the tiny apartment he'd gratefully claimed after three long days driving as fast as he could to get absolutely nowhere. A phone conversation with his father revealed he'd had a shadow the whole trip—a luxury travel trailer. They'd met at a twenty-four-hour diner, and Dean had to face the fact that if he'd really wanted to move on, he would've made it across the state line.

So he'd called Edna, emailed her links to some of his favorite, most devastating photos, the ones he was proudest of but that told the starkest stories, and took advantage of Edna's charity and sound advice.

When he wasn't busy feeling like a fool for leaving Elaine when she'd asked him to stay, he was dreaming up her response to this gamble.

Breaking down in front of friends and family would really embarrass him, but he'd take the chance because he had to stay here. He didn't want to dread meeting old friends.

Somehow this exhibition, the opportunity to tell his stories to Tall Pines, had become a test.

If he passed, nothing was holding him

back. He'd make plans for the future and convince Elaine she liked them, too.

If anyone could understand his need to make sense of both coming home and leaving his career behind to try something new, it was Elaine.

Edna handed him a glass of wine. "Drink up. It'll help."

He wasn't a wine kind of guy, but he didn't feel like arguing so he took her advice.

"Ready?" Edna asked as she smoothed her dark suit down her hips. His father took the plate out of his hand.

He thought about telling Edna he'd changed his mind, but then he saw Elaine run past the window toward the door. He couldn't quite see her through the crowd, but a small river parted and closed up until she appeared near the front.

"Ready." She was beautiful in the fancy dress, but her glasses and dark curls were familiar. It had been less than a week, but he'd missed her smiles. Right now, even her frown eased some of the worry he'd been living with ever since he left town.

She was here, and he would prove that he was never leaving again.

When he managed to look away from Elaine, everyone was looking at him. Edna's glare told him he'd missed his intro. She whispered, "No dead air!" and managed to work the wineglass out of his grasp.

Dean cleared his throat and glanced around the room, meeting eyes here and there until he found Elaine again. She was fussing with her hair, but her hands stilled as she nodded at him.

He needed her, and she was here.

"Thank you all for coming. Some of you are familiar, maybe from my first lifetime in Tall Pines or from my newest adventure, coming home. I convinced Edna to let me put together a show for the gallery's grand opening so that I could tell you all about what I've been doing while I've been away. These are stories that should be heard."

His dad crossed his arms over his chest, but the pride on his face beamed like a lighthouse across a rough sea.

Dean wasn't certain he could do this, but it was too important not to try.

He moved to stand in front of a black-

and-white photo of a soldier dressed in camouflage stretched out on the ground. One hand was behind his head and the other cradled a Father's Day card to his chest. Staring at the photo was painful, mainly because he'd taken it on the same trip that sent him home. The soldier could have died. A concussion seemed like a splinter in comparison, but they'd both lived. And Dean had come home. The soldier was still deployed, still forced to talk to his family through letters, emails and occasional phone calls. Every person that mattered to Dean was right here in this room. The least he could do was tell the story.

By the time he'd covered the six large photos of his travels, his chest ached, his voice was almost gone and more than one person in the crowd was in tears.

He glanced at Elaine to watch her wipe away a tear. She'd been…bedraggled when she came in. Now she was a red-eyed mess. Standing so close and yet too far away to wrap his arms around her was almost the hardest thing he'd done that evening. He watched her shoot uneasy glances to her left and right like she was making sure no one noticed. But he had.

"These stories matter," Dean said. "But they take a toll." He moved to stand in front of his photos of the Bluebird and downtown Tall Pines. These were the kinds of shots Edna wanted, souvenirs for tourists. They also told another important story. "And sometimes you have to come home to understand that toll. I can't imagine a better spot to recover."

He pointed at Elaine's wildflower photo, a beautiful shot of color next to his black-and-whites. "Sometimes you find beauty in the most unexpected locations. This was our Dr. Watson's first photography lesson."

The small wave of sound and the breeze as everyone turned to consider her was gratifying. She was fidgeting with her droopy curls again, but she'd regained a bit of her control.

"And this will be my next challenge. I'm going to teach photography lessons, maybe hold retreats, once the inn is up and running. We'll book weekend classes in the spring and fall. Anyone who'd like to learn how to tell a story through a lens can sign up. I want to make sure the stories that must be heard find their way to the world."

Everyone was quiet for a minute until Edna reminded them that all the photos were for sale. He wasn't sure what her cut was, but he had no doubt there was one. Before he could make his way to Elaine, his father wrapped his arms around him in a tight hug. "Good job. I'm so proud of you. And whatever I can do to help, I will." Before he could answer, Mark and Andrea were congratulating him. He reached around Andi to try to draw Elaine closer but she was gone.

MAKING A RUN for the privacy of the restroom had been a little cowardly, but it was absolutely necessary. Elaine ran her hands under the cold water and held her fingers over her eyes. She repeated the same move twice and then dried her face.

"Nothing is going to make those eyes look normal except time, Doctor," she muttered and tried to add some oomph to her hair.

Why was she fussing with her hair and makeup in the restroom?

Dean Collins had seen her at her worst: after a day of grimy renovation and limping through the woods. He wasn't going to change his mind about whatever he'd decided because her eyes were puffy and her nose red.

But losing his home might change that, no matter what he'd said before.

"You won't know how he feels until you talk to him." And she couldn't stay in the bathroom forever.

Although, as public restrooms went, it wouldn't be the worst place to hang out indefinitely.

A knock on the door jolted her back into the present. "Come out, Elaine. I know you're in there."

It was just Wanda Blankenship. She could bluff her way past Wanda. No problem.

After a deep breath, she pulled open the door, a wide smile on her face. "Wanda, I didn't know you're an art fan."

Wanda snorted. "I didn't know you owned more than one dress. Now I see it's at least two."

Elaine glanced at her dress and tried to

decide whether she should respond when Wanda had a valid point.

"At least it's a nice dress. Looks good on you." Wanda didn't smile. That made it seem more like a real compliment. First Edna. Now Wanda. It was a lot of unexpected kindness for one day.

"Here." Wanda held out a compact. "Use this."

Elaine opened it and swiped powder over the pink tip of her nose and her shiny cheeks. For half a second, she considered asking Wanda to apply eyeliner but changed her mind.

"You're going to tell us what happened tomorrow, aren't you? At Purl's Place?" Wanda asked as she dropped the compact into her purse. "That's the price of admission. The juiciest gossip you know. I have a hunch you'll take the prize. He was looking at you like you're a lost security blanket."

Again with the unexpected encouragement.

Elaine didn't know how long she stood there with her mouth open. Wanda finally gave her shoulder a nudge. "Come on. Everybody in the room could see it, two people who are going to be a whole lot better together than they ever were apart."

Elaine had been sitting on the dock for days, trying to solve this problem. Having Wanda Blankenship deliver it to her in the bathroom of the Tall Pines art gallery took some adjustment. "Wanda, you've just saved my life. Or my sanity anyway."

Wanda nodded and yanked open the door to usher Elaine out.

The crowd faded as Elaine worked her way across the gallery, her eyes locked on Dean. She was so proud of him. He may have thought he'd been admitting to weakness, but what he'd done tonight showed just how strong he was.

"Yeah, she's got a hold on the demo everywhere but the kitchen," Nick said, "but we'll have to start next week. Can't put it off much longer. Maybe the work will distract me from my heartbreak over postponing the marina." Nick sipped his drink. Andi must have given him a look because he said, "What? What did I say?"

"I wasn't sure what I was waiting for, but now I know," Elaine said and forced herself to hold her ground as the men turned to stare at her. "Dean, I need your help with one more project. Can you come out tomorrow?"

"I'd like that," Dean said and glowered at the circle surrounding them, sending a clear "beat it" message. "What's the hold up? Trouble at the bank?"

Elaine shrugged. "I couldn't quite get over the feeling that…" She took a deep breath. "Well, I was afraid the wrong person won." She pinched her nose when the sting of tears returned. "I didn't want to do anything that can't be undone. Not yet. But now I know exactly how to fix this."

Dean wrapped his hand around hers and pulled her to the corner. The whole room was still watching them, but it felt less exposed.

"What are you talking about?" Dean rested both hands on her shoulders. "You won because you have a solid plan, one that will attract families, all types of families." He snorted. "I was building my own clubhouse."

"How could you leave?" Elaine tangled her fingers together. "Never mind. I didn't mean to say that." Before he could answer, she said, "No, yes, I did. Why didn't you stay when I asked you to?" She shrugged off his hands. "I needed you to stay."

"And I needed some space. Just to figure out…" His gusty sigh made her realize she couldn't hear another trickle of conversation from anyone else. She checked over her shoulder and watched the frontline of the crowd spin around as though there was no way they'd been watching.

"I had to make sure this decision was going to stick," Dean said. "I needed to figure out who I was going to be now that I'm home."

"I should have dropped out of the competition." Elaine squeezed her hands together. "My practice here is enough, and I want you to stay."

Dean narrowed his eyes and then slowly said, "You… You would give up? You're going to…give me a pity win? Forfeit the game?"

"No, not now. What I have is even better, but I need you to stay. I need to know you're safe. I want you to have the dock when you need it. I only want…" *You to be happy.* She couldn't say it, but she had the feeling he understood anyway. "Please. Meet me on the dock tomorrow."

Ignoring the crowd, he bent and pressed a kiss against her lips. She had to smile at the low "aww" that swept through the crowd.

And for the first time since he'd walked away, she was certain. The upsetting confusion was gone. She was going to get everything she wanted.

DEAN PARKED NEXT to the giant tree in front of the Bluebird, Elaine's car in what he'd started to think of as her usual spot. He slid out and studied the building for a minute, happy it looked just as beautiful as it always did in his memories.

He owed that to Elaine.

She didn't call him or turn, but he could see her standing at the end of the dock and the anxiety—the tension that had started to fray his nerves the minute she'd asked him to stay and he'd left—finally settled. Dean slowly walked to meet her.

"First, I want to apologize," Dean said as he sat next to her. "I should have explained that I just needed time. I always intended to come back, but I wanted to have myself together. That's been my struggle all along."

Elaine held out a small binder. "As grand gestures go, beginning with an art show and ending with a kiss was impressive." Then she smiled. "It's nice to know you have the romantic gesture in you, but a phone call would have worked just as well."

"Not for me. The biggest mistakes deserve the best apologies." He bumped her shoulder. "In case you missed it, I'm extremely sorry I reacted the same way I always have when things are overwhelming. All I need is this spot. And you."

She nodded. "It's nice to hear that as I have a solid business proposal for you, one I wouldn't trust to just anyone. No, the partner I want has to love the Bluebird. And if he decides to skip town, I will ask Jackie for his attorney recommendation." She narrowed her eyes at him, but her lips were twitching. He took the binder she was holding.

"Why do I have a feeling that I'm about to lose another race I didn't know we were running?" He slowly opened the binder. On the front was a picture of the cove with a drawing of a beautiful marina. It was nothing like the bare bones one he'd proposed.

The building itself was split in two parts, one next to the boat slips with gas pumps out front and a small window for sales. The other side, the one facing the lake, had walls of giant windows. "Is this a restaurant?" He thought he could see a few tables on the drawing.

"Yes. Or a grill. Whatever you think is best." Elaine trailed her feet through the water.

"So this is your plan for next year?" Dean turned the pages and studied her information. Her outline was sketchier than the forecast he'd pulled together, but she'd included bids from Nick.

"Or this year. Whenever you can get it done." She shrugged. "I'll handle the inn. You work on the marina." She turned her head to look at him. "Together, we're going to build an amazing place."

Dean looked out over the cove while he considered her plan. Moving it out would cost more, but the view in front would remain almost untouched. He'd have to work with his father over the details of who would own that land, but the location was better. The business would be brisker. And she was absolutely right.

When he turned to say so, she just nodded. "I know. Brilliant, right? I can't help it. It just comes to me." She rolled her eyes. "And Wanda Blankenship will never let me hear the end of this, especially after I smoke her in the next race."

He flipped slowly through the pages again. "But you could have it all. To yourself. Just like you imagined."

"Or I could get smarter, realize the first plan sometimes needs adjustments." She smiled up at him. "This place, it doesn't work without you. No matter what happens in the future, the Collins men belong here. And I need to know you're safe. Then I can be happy." She blinked rapidly.

"You know what I need?" Dean brushed her curls away from her face and straightened her glasses. "Time to prove I mean what I say when I promise I'm never going to leave you. Ever. Not when you run off in the woods. Not when you beat me at a race I don't know we're running. Not when you work too hard or too long. Bluebird or not, I'm not leaving you. I need you, and I'm sure I always will. I was confused, forgot for a minute that home was about more than the building. I have plans. You're in them. The Bluebird is in them. And if we can work this out, that marina is going to rock."

She threw her arms around his neck. "Fine, but don't forget to schedule some time for all the climbing and hiking and death-defying stunts I'm going to hire you for. I want to do a kid's science camp and maybe a survival skills weekend now and then. I won't be able to do it all myself."

Dean frowned as he considered that. "Sure, I can see taking a small group of boys out, showing them some basics, maybe camping overnight."

"Actually, I was thinking girls." She shrugged. "But both is the right answer."

"There could be a lot of giggling," Dean murmured. "I might have to charge more."

"Just tell the boys to keep it down," she said and rolled her eyes. "Hailey and her friends, they're going to show you."

"And you, Dr. Watson," Dean said as he pulled her closer, "will you be joining us?

I could show you how to tell north from south. Maybe keep you from getting lost."

"It's a good thing I love you, Dean Collins," Elaine murmured as she moved closer to press her lips against his. "You'll have to remind me why when I forget."

Before Dean could reply, they heard a low-pitched warble. Elaine smiled and squeezed her eyes shut. "That's a bluebird, right? They're back. I thought I heard them earlier this week, but I wasn't sure. What do you think did the trick?"

"Elementary, my dear Dr. Watson." Dean laughed as she rolled her eyes. "They came home."

EPILOGUE

Six months later

"I NEVER WOULD'VE thought my mom could have a second career as a wedding planner. Who knew she could take on bridezillas and win?" Elaine ducked behind Dean when her mother turned toward them. She'd been fussing with table settings for ages. Every guest had a full place setting. That would have to be good enough.

"It's scary how skilled she is at this." Dean pulled her arms around his middle and waved cheerfully at her mother.

"I know. It's another 'solid revenue stream' or so Edna says." She rested her forehead on his back and closed her eyes. "I think you're right about hiring someone to help me keep track of all these streams of income. Your adventure tours. My kids' camps. Now the wedding venue my mother has carved out of white picket fence and the new gazebo. It's a lot."

Dean turned and pulled her against his chest. She straightened his pale blue tie. "You really do clean up nice."

He nodded. "I know."

"Stop standing around and grinning at each other," her mother snapped as she trotted up the front steps. "Andi and Mark deserve a perfect wedding. Get a move on. Go make sure the cabin's prepared." She disappeared inside, and Dean tugged Elaine's hand until she followed him down the steps.

"Are we running away?" Elaine said. "Do you have the keys to the RV? Your dad will never miss it." She laughed as she hurried to keep up with him.

"As long as we don't steal the boat, we'd get a sound head start, but first I want to show you something." Elaine checked over her shoulder to be certain her mother couldn't see them.

"Look." He pointed at a bright blue flower. "The morning glory seeds you planted. The vines are blooming." He pressed a sweet kiss against her lips. "Thank you for bringing back the flowers and the birds and everything about this place that made it so special."

"We did it. Together." Elaine wanted to say the right thing, but she couldn't. He was everything she'd been looking for without realizing it.

"You know, I think I'm going to cry." Elaine blinked rapidly. "I don't want to, but I am."

Dean straightened his tie, the one he'd been fidgeting with all day. It was his only tie, actually. Hiking, climbing, running, fishing, none of them required business attire. "All right. I have a problem we need to solve. That will help, right?"

"I hope so." Elaine sniffed. Dean knelt on the grass, and she almost warned him about stains but she'd been really trying to get control of her bossy voice lately. He picked up a stick like he was about to draw a diagram so she bent to see better.

"Here's what I'm wondering. If we run away to Vegas, will your mother change the locks? Lead a mutiny against us?" He shook his head. "She's the best wedding planner around."

Elaine frowned and then covered her mouth with both hands when he pulled out a diamond ring. She had to take deep breaths before she said, "Yeah, she's good with revenge. I'm not sure I'd want to go to war with her."

Dean frowned. "I guess we'll have to get married here, then. At least we know how to do it now."

Elaine couldn't look away from his face as images of their future floated through her mind. They'd argue over painting and repairs and expansion. His father would fillet fish from their beautiful new gazebo. Her mother would hunt them down anytime she needed boots on the ground. They'd probably have a daughter that broke every bone in her body and a son who collected rocks in his pockets. And they'd end every day rocking on the front porch.

She couldn't answer him. She held out her hand.

"So that's a yes?" Dean slipped the ring on her finger, and the crowd that had gathered behind them, no doubt marshaled by her mother, erupted in cheers. Edna was there with pink hair to match her pink floral dress. Sue and all the Shady Ladies watched from the front porch. Elaine could hear Andi cheering from the second-floor window.

"Now then, let's race to the cabin. Want to? I'll even let you win."

Elaine was laughing too hard to see as she ran behind him, trusting him to get them where they needed to be.

* * * * *

*You're always welcome in
the town of Tall Pines!
Don't miss A MINUTE ON THE LIPS,
the first book in Cheryl Harper's
WELCOME TO TALL PINES
miniseries, available now!*

LARGER-PRINT BOOKS!

GET 2 FREE LARGER-PRINT NOVELS PLUS 2 FREE MYSTERY GIFTS

Love Inspired®

Larger-print novels are now available...

REQUEST YOUR FREE BOOKS!

2 FREE RIVETING INSPIRATIONAL NOVELS
PLUS 2 FREE MYSTERY GIFTS

Love Inspired®
SUSPENSE

ReaderService.com

Manage your account online!

- Review your order history
- Manage your payments
- Update your address

---

*We've designed
the Harlequin® Reader Service
website just for you.*

Enjoy all the features!

- Reader excerpts from any series
- Respond to mailings and
  special monthly offers
- Discover new series available to you
- Browse the Bonus Bucks catalog
- Share your feedback

Visit us at:
ReaderService.com